Buck's Night:

Destination Earth

by

Jayne Collett

Buck's Night:Destination Earth
Copyright © 2024 Jayne Collett

Collett, Jayne.
Buck's Night:Destination Earth.

ISBN: 9781763540620

Cover and interior design by Jayne Collett

Buy a paperback or eBook from Amazon

For my family.
The best party animals ever!

LET'S PAAAAAARRRRTTTYYY!!!!!

WHEN: Saturday, 7.00 p.m.

WHERE: Stardust Foyer.

WHY: Kiss goodbye to Marc's balls.

DESTINATION: Any place with booze, women and booze.

RULE 1: No using four letter words such as 'love' and 'wife'.

RULE 2: Alcohol is your best friend.

RULE 3: Drinks must be guzzled as quickly as possible.

RULE 4: Every attempt must be made to break the current drinking record. Any man not giving his fullest effort to the record will be tortured.

RULE 5: Two of the same drink cannot be consumed in a row.

RULE 6: If you throw up, your drink tally goes back to zero.

RULE 7: If you drop it - you mop it.

RULE 8: Two words: Respect and Consideration. (Use a dictionary if you have to).

RULE FOR ANYONE WHO USED A DICTIONARY: Stay home.

RULE FOR ANYONE WHO DOESN'T LIKE THE RULES: Put on a dress, stay home with your mother and bake.

Saturday. 7 o'clock.
Weather: Clear, warm and cloud free.
Transportation - check. Drinks - check. Entertainment – check.
Brains locked into party mode – check.

The guys stood in the foyer of the Stardust waiting for Marc. He was late. It may have only been by five minutes but in the history of buck's nights it was unheard of. No man, who was soon to become the recipient of a homing device, had ever been late. Such behaviour was considered unnatural.

Joc felt slightly apprehensive. He imagined a giant thumb bearing down on Marc, pinning him helplessly to the floor as every woman within a five kilometre radius lectured him about concepts he was yet to master, such as responsibility and common sense. Don't drink too much, they were probably saying, and don't do anything stupid. Throw in a bit about trust and fidelity and how guilt eventually kills and boom, a man's conscience could be seriously compromised. Girlie emotions were a dangerous thing and good men had been lost to them before today.

For a moment Joc considered leaving without him. If Marc's mind had been tainted he'd be about as much fun as a chess player on Prozac. Ordinarily the others would have agreed and happily gotten drunk in Marc's honour but he wasn't late enough just yet to warrant abandoning him and they still had the 'kidnap him kicking and screaming' option.

Joc wandered over to the doors and stared out at the parking lot looking for any sign of a dazed and confused eunuch. Nothing. "He's not gonna show," he said, totally convinced.

"Maybe he's scared, you know, 'cos of Sumo," Kam suggested, shooting a quick glance in Sumo's direction. Poor bastard, he thought.

"He's getting married! What's scarier than that, for crying out loud," Phil said.

"Lena," Davis said, feigning fear and holding up his hands as if to ward off evil. "You've seen the way she looks at me, checking me out like I'm a prime piece of meat; good husband material."

Harri shook his head. "It's physically impossible for Lena to 'check you out'. One eye heads southeast while the other heads northwest. You gotta run back and forth in front of her just to say hello."

Ha, ha, ha.

Oh yeah, they could afford to make fun. They weren't old, lonely and desperate - yet.

The foyer doors opened and Marc rushed in. His cheeks were flushed.

"Well look who finally decided to show," Joc said.

"Settle down, I'm only a coupla minutes late."

"Did anyone try and give you the 'morals/ethics' talk?" Joc wanted to check before they set off - just in case they needed to leave him after all.

"Nah. I'm still a complete man."

A dozen responses went unvoiced because no one could be bothered stating the obvious.

Marc slapped Sumo on the back. "Big fella, glad you could make it. You're lookin'… hey, you're lookin' and that's always a good sign."

Sumo was looking, all right. Sumo was looking relieved. Hints had been dropped to the effect that if Marc had been prematurely emasculated the guys would make him the proxy, and he wasn't about to go through that hell again. Ever.

"Let's go then," Joc rubbed his hands eagerly. "While we're still young enough."

The guys made their way across the parking lot and quickly piled into the 'look after it with your life or have your gonads cut off' cruiser.

The cruiser belonged to Phil's old man and it was sleek; it was smooth; it was easy to park and it was sparkling white with silver chrome that was polished so hard it made your eyes hurt to look at it. Not only did Phil's old man have a thing for shiny metal he also had a thing for lights. Like some people loved air horns, he loved luminescence. Nearly every available space on the vehicle had a light - blue, red, yellow, green, orange, but his favourite was the bright white one underneath the body. When it was turned on it made everything glow and the cruiser looked as if it was doing just that - cruising; skimming over the terrain, never touching the ground. He knew the neighbours were jealous of that beauty.

As they entered the vehicle the party mood was high. If Phil's old man hadn't come through with transport they would have been stuck doing something at the back of Joc's place which, when all was said and done, wouldn't have been much at all. The guys wanted to give Marc a decent send off before his responsibility gene was forcefully activated. It was the least they could do. As far as they were concerned, after marriage all you had were your memories and it was up to your friends to concoct a few good ones because, if all went to plan, the groom wouldn't remember a thing.

Marc looked around the cruiser in awe. Phil's old man must have recently traded up. "How much your old man get this for?" he asked.

Phil settled into the driver's seat. "Nothin'. He spotted it one night, radioed 'Shifty's Tow' and had it hauled home. The thing had just been dumped."

Yeah right!

Before Phil started the engine he turned his attention to address the others. "OK, here's the rules - don't put any marks on the leather and if you wanna puke or take a leak, use the toilet like you're s'posed to."

"What are we - animals?" Tash said.

"I wish. They got better manners," Phil said. "It's my arse on the line so show a bit of respect."

Phil fired up the cruiser and the soft, gentle hum of the engine brought with it a promise of good things to come. No way could they have a bad time and no way were they going to. The cruiser glided along the road as smooth as silk. The hands of the transport God had tuned this machine to perfection. Nothing could disturb its balance, its uncomplicated movement forward into the unknown night. Gracefully, and without a sound, it lifted up into the sky. Ten, twenty, thirty thousand feet with no effort at all, leaving their home planet of Dectarus way behind.

Marc ran a finger over the radar screen as Phil worked the instruments. Phil's old man had turned an all time classic into the most up to date machine he'd ever seen. The cruiser had originated on the planet Cadill about two hundred years before and the design proved so popular imitations soon cropped up all over the place. Earth called their version a Cadillac. That was the thing about innovative designs and ideas, they had a way of crossing the boundaries of the universe. If a suitable deal (usually involving graft, corruption, and snack foods), could be made between the interested parties then technology was happily shared.

Marc looked at the blinking this and the flashing that and thought about his father's broken down bomb which clunked and lurched so violently you always kicked yourself in the head on take off. And his father wondered why he didn't want to use it for wedding transport. As if weddings weren't painful enough!

The wedding thought made Marc's mouth go dry. Suddenly and urgently he needed a drink. He dragged himself away from the flashy instrument panel and joined the others at the rear of the cruiser where they were taking full advantage of the plush and roomy interior by sprawling themselves out untidily.

Kam was behind the bar. He'd been put in charge of drinks because he had a habit of screwing up ingredients and measures, which suited everyone just fine. Usually you got something so potent that, if by some miracle it didn't kill you, it would eat away any decay in your teeth.

The bar was definitely the cruiser's most outstanding feature. It contained at least one bottle of every kind of alcoholic drink and a computerised book containing recipes collected from seventy-five different planets over a two year period. Some had come through via mail order while others had been collected personally. Harri had provided a few extra cans of cheap, local stuff but they pretty much had the run of the bar. Phil's old man appreciated the need for a man to drink. Anyway, Phil's old man hadn't paid for the booze.

Kam's potions were going down nice and easy and he worked steadily to have drinks made, and ready to go, before they were even wanted; each concoction different from the one before. He took a shot of Protto with a Carvit Chaser. His heart stopped beating and his legs gave way. When he hit the floor his vitals restarted. He jumped up and carried on as if nothing had happened.

Music thumped away in the background, largely ignored by the guys because they were all caught up in conversation. Only Sumo sat quietly, seemingly lost in his thoughts.

Marc nudged Joc, "Check him out, I think we've lost him already."

"Give him a chance. He'll come good. Bet you're glad you weren't the one getting married when we stopped off at Tourdefra. One non-alcoholic mixer..." Joc shook his head sympathetically. "I'm amazed Sotty still married him."

"He's getting better though. He can string a full sentence together now." Marc really, really hoped he wouldn't end up like Sumo.

Part of Sumo's trouble was that he actually remembered his buck's night. It would come back in flashes - Intoe, and his sagging, wrinkled man-boob with its six multi-coloured nipples. The grossly out-of-fashion dress made from puce taffeta he'd been forced to wear while Intoe paraded him up and down the strip looking for business; the business he'd been forced to honour; the brightly coloured disease that saw his nuts end up in a sling; the drink that proved nearly fatal because its alcohol content had been carelessly diluted with a fruit juice mixer and the visiting Ketolian who wanted to take him home as her pet because of the "adorable hair above his eyes."

Sumo knew the only thing that saved him was lapsing into a coma and conveniently coming around just in time for the wedding the following week. After those experiences he felt it was his right to stare into space, twitch at the memories and drink loads of booze to help him forget.

He gulped down his Triple Fronty Hiball and it must have oiled the cogs in his brain because the voices of the guys began disturbing his languor. He could hear Davis bleating about his run in with the Razor Toothed Redfin that had thoughtlessly bitten off most of his impregnator. Loser!

"The lab are working on growing me another one. I think." Davis sounded a little unsure.

"Why should the lab grow you anything? Kam's worse off than you," Joc declared. "He's been missing brain bits for ages because the public health system don't consider his case a high priority. D'ya really think growing you a couple of inches of flaccid skin is on top of their 'to do' list?"

"Especially when it'll never get used anyway," said Sumo. He spoke. The Grenyth Tomb was loosening him up.

"You'd know all about that, now you're married," Davis shot back.

Phil had set the cruiser on auto and came to the back of the cabin to hang with the others. He grabbed a Juripet Melon-V with a Sprig Twister and sat next to Sumo.

His tic working overtime, Sumo spoke again. "Are we going back to Tourdefra?"

"Relax, big fella," Phil said, "we're not heading for that part of the galaxy tonight. I thought we'd buzz Earth."

"Earth! Will we be welcome there?" Davis asked nervously. "Should we signal ahead that we're coming 'cos I don't want any trouble."

"There won't be any trouble. The Guide says it's mostly harmless and my old man reckons the main thing they worry about is being invaded and taken over by hideous space creatures who'll control their minds and destroy them. Shit, we're only going for a night out. That's hardly a threat. Besides, we're not welcome on any of the good planets so, Earth it is. We'll be there shortly," he told them.

The guys could comfortably hang around Earth and not be too conspicuous because fortunately, or unfortunately, depending on how you looked at it, of all the life forms on all the planets and star systems in the galaxy the Dectarians looked most like Earthlings. There were a few minor differences, but nothing too noticeable. They had no eyebrows or fingernails, twenty-four teeth, a telepathy knob behind their right ear, they used ninety-two percent of their brain capacity (except for Kam who now possessed only two-thirds of his brain due to a most unfortunate accident on Tylamar), and they never got acne.

They also used the same concepts of measuring time as the Earthlings. Their culture was similar, just further advanced, and most importantly of all they knew nothing about diets, banks, politics, or religion; four money making institutions that had long ago been outlawed due to the unnecessary stress and animosity caused by them. They were definitely a more relaxed and jovial people because of this.

To Earth's credit, a recent poll by 'Rocks, Shiny Objects and Liquid Matter' magazine had voted it the ninth most visually attractive planet from a distance of four hundred kilometres or more because of its lovely green and blue hues. But even with that award under its belt, Earth and its residents were actually safe from invasion by beings from other planets, stars and solar systems. This was because the water wasn't drinkable and Earthlings were perceived as being snobs by the other races.

Because they never visited anywhere else in the universe, preferring to confine themselves to their own little world, the other races had no interest in holidaying on Earth and spending their hard earned money at a place that continually snubbed them. The fact that they weren't capable of travelling anywhere was largely beside the point. The other races had overcome that problem millennia ago and reasoned that Earth should be up to speed by now.

Earth did have fly-by-nighters come in every now and then, but they made sure never to boost the economy in any way by spending anything. Usually they came by for a quick look around or to snaffle something from the planet they couldn't get anywhere else. Often it was used as a stop over on the way to or from another destination and it was a good, quiet place to catch forty winks before moving on. Contrary to popular belief by humans, the planet was used mostly as a convenience stop. They were the restroom of the universe.

Some annoyance for Earth and its people also stemmed from the fact that, besides the small planet of Carfang, Earth was the only place in the universe that cut things down and dug things up in an effort to learn how their planet came to be, how long it had been there and how much longer it was likely to last. Wilful abuse of a harmless bit of rock was considered by many to be in extremely poor taste and not terribly kind.

The irony of the mindless destruction was that not four light years away, in a library on Seesayer, there was a book that gave all the answers to all the most oft asked questions like 'What's for dinner?' and 'Why am I here?' It was an old volume containing the wisdom of the ages and the much sought solution to why a certain chicken crossed the road. All in all it was a very informative piece of work. It would take no more than three hours to read and every explanation sought for all things considered a mystery were answered in plain and simple language that even a child could understand. The entire history of the planet, from its formation to the various life forms it had contained, was there for the taking but the book sat patiently, day after day, year after year, waiting for someone to come along and, with a nice hot cup of tea and a few hours to spare, go through it. But no one ever came.

When the compiler of the book was originally offered the task of jotting down Earth's history he had unkindly answered "ZGF*#DE!!" which, roughly translated, meant "Don't insult my intelligence with such a trivial matter." However, the money offered was too good to refuse, besides which it would help pay off a few gambling debts and get him a bottle or three of Sweet Peach Cider which his wife claimed he loved more than her. An observation not without a degree of accuracy.

So C. S. Hexxwernan got to work. He wrote on all subjects from the landmarks in the Middle East to the fossilised remains of artefacts to the creative concept of God and some of its associated matters - i.e.: Church collection plates and Christmas as a time of commercial greed, right up to humankind being a malformed accident that should have remained a pile of buffalo faeces had it not been for the accidental event of a lemming/skunk hybrid, looking for a warm place to sleep one night, inadvertently becoming trapped in the sticky goo and somehow mutating into the present form of the human.

Notions that had been commonly held by Earthlings for centuries were shot to pieces as bad guesses and ill-informed conjecture and much lauded scientific hypotheses were highlighted and corrected, where the theories had gone wrong, with the flourish of a bright red pen.

Hexxwernan loved using his pen to carve up the inept ideas of those he considered to be lesser beings and, as it turned out, it was an easy book to write as the history was straight-forward and easily explainable. To Hexxwernan, his fee was like getting money for nothing and he laughed all the way to the racetrack.

Chapter Two

As the cruiser travelled through space, and thousands of light years whizzed on by, Kam threw chunks of ice into the crusher and stared with wonder and awe as it turned the blocks into snowflakes. Davis wandered over to the bar and watched the process with matched glee. Phil made a move to join them.

Joc's features elicited disbelief as he watched Davis and Kam having a wonderful time with an electrical appliance. "What are you fairies doing?" he said. "Hey guys, check out the ice queens."

A little too quickly, Phil relaxed back into his seat then fidgeted exaggeratedly as if he'd only originally moved because of some great discomfort. He felt most put out that he wouldn't get to see the crusher in action. He tried to mask his disappointment. "Yeah, is this a buck's night or a ladies kitchen party?"

Marc stood up and headed for the bar.

"You going to check out the crusher too?" Phil asked, adding some fake laughter for Joc's benefit.

"I'm getting a drink," Marc answered, holding up his empty glass.

Phil nearly hit himself for not thinking of that. He quickly swallowed the contents of his glass and followed Marc's lead. To avert suspicion about their true motives, Sumo and Harri casually strolled to the bar, stopping for a brief moment to discuss the tasteful decor.

Joc shook his head then pointed at Tash who, thankfully, had stayed seated. "Did you get us any entertainment?"

"Yeah." Tash sprang to life. "My brother lent me a couple of discs he got from Ellitas. They're kinda interactive." He sloshed his drink as he stood up. "I don't know what they're like but Rodge reckons they're hot. He usually picks good stuff."

"Will you girls be joining us?" Joc lisped at the six grown men who were now fighting over whose turn it was to add ice to the machine.

"Just getting a drink. There in a tick," Phil said. He poured himself a Mamomile Lotion with Pane Juice and realised too late the two should never be mixed. He now had a drink that tasted like the sweat from a mating camel.

Tash put one of the discs into the image projection unit and a 3-D holographic image popped up in the middle of the floor. A woman with a wrinkled forehead and three wisps of hair stood uneasily on shoes with seven inch platforms. Anatomically she wasn't all that different from Dectarian women. A few minor differences, but nothing terribly unusual.

"Knockers," Sumo yelled excitedly. The ice crusher could no longer compete.

Kam was deserted; bums filled seats and drool dribbled. The guys cheered the image and yelled, "Strip."

With a bored expression on her face, and stifling a yawn, the woman started to move gracelessly. From somewhere within the picture, music started. The guys cheered her on as if she was the most exotic and sensuous being in the universe. And the rate in which they were pouring drinks down their throats had managed to make her just that.

The apathetic stripper slowly began to undress. The image moved closer to the guys. In a language that was unfamiliar she asked what the occasion was. They thought she must have been talking dirty and cheered more. Unable to communicate she decided to work the room. Don't leave any of 'em out, that was the best option. Anyway, it'd give them something to talk about tomorrow as they nursed their hangovers.

As she went from one to the other and slowly peeled her clothes off she recited her shopping list in a husky voice. They couldn't understand a word so she figured - who cares. She made rude gestures with her mouth and fingers, whilst muttering something about memory suppressants and gin. The guys' eyes were bugging out of their heads. When she got to Marc the cheering became more intense. From this she figured he was the main one to focus on.

She extended her hand toward him and invited him to stand. The others pushed his body out of the chair. He fell forward and landed at her right feet. He noticed the ends of the toes were painted. One set were blue and the other black. It was the same on the left feet. This meant she was an especially lewd hologram. Marc thought that was a good thing, under the circumstances. She rubbed her body up and down Marc's. He could feel her every lump and bump; her fingers undoing his jeans. Even though she was only a hologram, she was part of a very sophisticated system.

Holographic discs were big business in many parts of the universe. The sophistication of the programmes were the result of many years of hard work by a Philgian female who was sick of her husband. She wanted the companionship of marriage without all the other crap that went with it.

Eating her breakfast one morning she wished her husband had a volume switch because the noises he was making whilst shovelling food down his throat were setting her nerves on edge. The fat bastard also had a permanently blocked nose so he had to breathe through his mouth and chew at the same time; a sound not recommended for those with sensitive stomachs or inclinations towards psychotic episodes. She knew she had but two options - kill him outright or trade him in on something better.

If she murdered him her subscription to 'Furry Creatures as Centre Pieces' would be cancelled and trading him up for a new, improved model didn't guarantee happiness. Neither choice was sound. Then it came to her - if she could create an image that could be projected anywhere, was solid in nature, had the ability to think, speak and rationalise, do as was asked without argument or dissension and could be turned on and off whenever it suited, she'd be onto a guaranteed winner.

And she was! Initially, coming up with the software to manifest solid images out of coherent light was a problem but the more meals she shared with her husband, the harder she worked on the task. She bought every available piece of technology from the most advanced societies and integrated the best ideas to create a working model. Why nobody had thought of the concept sooner was beyond her. It seemed such an obvious step towards much needed happiness and contentment.

Then, one bright afternoon, on the first third of the planet's rotation around the orange star of warmth, it happened - her hologram came to life. She put it through its paces immediately. It did the dishes, it romanced her, it agreed with everything she said even if it knew she was wrong, it didn't make any hideous bodily noises and best of all it didn't need to eat so she didn't have to cook for it and then listen to its slobbering. It was perfect.

The moment the discs became available they were snapped up. Females everywhere threw out their husbands and got themselves a 3D image of light that had more life in it than the real thing and the glorious holograms were so advanced the only thing they couldn't do was produce offspring. The images themselves believed they were alive and living real lives and so planned various activities they thought they might need to do in order to survive day to day, but they could only really do what they were specifically programmed for.

As the company grew, so did the ideas. Not only did she produce husbands, she produced wives, well-behaved children and obedient teenagers. She was the toast of the system. By using pictures from magazines, from as many planets as she could, she created quite a catalogue of looks, shapes and sizes to cater for all tastes, races and kinky fetishes. The variety was huge.

But branching out into the entertainment industry was her greatest achievement. That was really where her success lay and that was where she made the most money, becoming famous on sixty-seven percent of the universe's habitable rocks. Home shopping, craft tips, exercise, taxidermy, painting by numbers; you name it, it was available but it was sex and titillation that were the huge, huge sellers. From a single strip tease, to a full-on orgy involving anything with a tongue or an orifice, the discs always sold out in the blink of an eye. They were even more popular than croquet tournaments, and that was really saying something. Yep, she was a genius, and a rich one at that, and all because her now ex-husband was a slob. Necessity was certainly the mother of invention.

Marc stood motionless while the lustful, luscious, lady of light did all the work, caressing his body with her feathery touch, whispering softly, probably about how she'd love to screw him or something like that. He grinned at the guys. Tash had done good. She was reminding herself to pick up tissues and face cream.

Just as her hand was reaching into the front of Marc's jeans there was a loud bang and the cruiser jolted. Her image flickered out. It came back up but the programme had gone back to the start. She was fully dressed and teetering uneasily. Marc was on the floor wondering what had happened. The guys had stopped cheering and were looking at each other.

"What have you done, Kam?" Joc shouted. "Did you touch something?"

Before Kam had a chance to reply, Phil leapt out of his seat and rushed to the controls. The display told him that the left side of the cruiser had been hit by a hurtling rock. There was a tear in the metal and several dents.

"My old man's gonna go viral," said Phil, who had gone a greenish colour. And it wasn't just the booze making his stomach churn.

"Will it still fly OK?" Marc asked.

"That's not a problem. But how am I gonna explain this to him. He'll never let me use it again."

"How can you control what flying rocks do? Anyway, don't worry, we'll just take it to the Stardust when we get back," Joc said.

"Sure! You need to book a month ahead for that place and I don't have a month."

"Relax," said Joc. "I already took care of that ages ago, just in case we might have needed it. E.P. will be waiting for us."

Phil relaxed immediately. The Stardust used to be a flea-ridden bar where people got killed just for wearing the wrong shoes. E.P. came along and transformed the place into one of the best bar and grill's this side of the Darley Haverson Nebula. As a sideline it also had the most famous panel beating shop in three galaxies. Its specialty was dealing with buck's night revellers who undoubtedly came home with trashed up vehicles. They could sober up or further drink themselves into oblivion while they waited. It was a very lucrative business.

With that little problem fixed they grabbed another round of drinks and brought their attention back to the stripper. She stood there quietly. Without initial instruction she didn't operate.

Sumo, who'd been slumped over for the last five minutes owing to sensory overload brought on by the excitement of seeing a naked woman, suddenly sat bolt upright. "Can you guys hear those voices?" he asked.

"That's just the booze talking, or else you're possessed," Harri said.

"Nah, he's right," said Phil. "Listen."

They all stood still and concentrated on hearing what the other two had. Sure enough, there was a murmuring interspersed with occasional voices.

"What is that?" said Tash.

They stood there for a moment longer trying to figure it out. Joc reached behind his right ear and fiddled with his telepathy switch. All he could hear now was the blender mixing up a Yellow Tyraid Frist. "We must have entered Earth's atmosphere," he said, "'cos we're picking up on thoughts. Turn your switches off."

They all did as Joc suggested because, at the distance they were at, there was no point trying to hone in on any one person. To attempt to get anything discernible was near impossible unless they were virtually on top of someone.

The vehicle was cruising Earth's sky at an altitude of five thousand feet. From their vantage point the Earth looked quiet and still. If they were that distance above Kryzon they would have heard music playing and parties going on from every bit of land mass. The guys would have gone there, but they'd been banned.

Phil pointed at the seats proudly. "My old man got this leather from Earth. He picked up a few cows he saw roaming around a field. Said they'd just been abandoned."

"What's a cow?" Marc asked.

"It's like a cudfer, only bigger."

"They're so cute," Sumo enthused.

"It's good quality, and soft too," Harri said, fingering the leather. "I've never seen anything like it."

"You can only get it from Earth," Phil said proudly.

"Not anymore. 'Hide and Sneak' won a contract to harvest it," Davis informed them, "so it's now available on Western Bluff. That means there'll be no more illegal hijacking."

"I feel sorry for the cows," Kam announced as he offered up fresh drinks, "because their insides fall out when their skin's removed."

"That's such a shame," Sumo said. His voice was thick with emotion.

The others nodded in sympathy and suddenly became devastatingly interested in the leather and wondered how it got such a nice smell. Did it need polishing? What colours did it come in? Could you wear it? Could they get some without hurting the cows? Did the cows have families?

Joc and Tash stood back and watched six grown men exposing and sharing their emotions. The ice crusher was one thing, this was quite another.

"Ladies."

No response.

"Ladies!" Joc snapped. "You've just spent the last half hour farting on that dead animal so get over it and move on. Now, before I die of boredom, could we please return our focus to the important stuff."

"Does anybody remember why we're here?" Tash added.

"Yeah," Harri said defensively. "Booze and women."

"Very good Harri. There will be a door prize for you." Joc's voice dripped with sarcasm. "So, where are we going?"

"To where booze and women are," Sumo roared. The others cheered their assent. They were back. The leather could no longer compete.

Hallelujah for short attention spans, thought Joc. "Phil, display the map."

The home screen, which was flashing with a psychedelic urgency the words ꞁEARTH YEAR 1996ꞁ, was replaced by a global map. Because they knew next to nothing about the sleeping planet below, they decided to circle the globe in a purely random fashion then bring the cruiser to a screaming halt. Whichever country they were above, they'd go there.

With another drink each and another brain cell or ten on its last legs they sat back and let the cruiser take them wherever it chose.

"Tash, put the other disc in while we wait," said Marc. "We'll come back to the stripper later."

"OK, this one's a movie. It's interactive as well."

The guys made howling sounds and grunted to show their approval. Tash swapped the discs over.

Soft, soothing music filled the cabin. A woman of what looked like Gremisan origin appeared in the middle of the floor. She had a weak chin, no neck and a middle age perm, but to the guys she was one tetra looking babe. She smiled sweetly and spoke. "Thank you for joining us ladies. Today we're going to show you how to knit a lovely tea cosy for your favourite pot. They're also ideal as gifts or just as a give-away for that someone special. First you will need two …"

The guys sat there stunned. What the hell was this? She wasn't getting naked; she wasn't rolling around with several people moaning and saying, 'Oh yeah, give it to me'. She wasn't inviting the guys to join her. She was talking knitting. Knitting!

Tash dived for the projection unit and ripped the disc out before their minds turned soft. He'd get his brother for this. He turned back to his friends and laughed nervously. "Ha, ha. Rodge must've slipped me the wrong one. Ha, ha."

Joc stood up and started towards him. "I give you one lousy job, one lousy stinking job to do and you stuff it up. 'Take care of the entertainment', I say. 'Hey, no problem', you say. 'Can you get some good stuff', I say. 'Hey, no problem', you say. And look what you got, your mother's knitting show."

"It's Rodge's fault. He told me it'd really get us going."

"Well he wasn't wrong there," Marc said.

"We still got the stripper," Tash offered feebly.

"Yeah," slurred Sumo, "I think she really liked me."

"How would you know," said Joc, "you weren't even conscious when she was on." He shook his head and tutted irritably. "Put the brakes on Phil, and let's go down to the surface. Maybe we can pick up something for the trip home."

Phil went up front and messed around with a few switches. The cruiser stopped dead. The land scanner brought their location up onto the screen.

"According to this," Phil said, "we're above a place called Siberia. I'll scan for the co-ordinates of where there's the most activity and we can just cruise straight down."

While the guys waited for Phil to do his thing they had another drink. Then another. Phil was certainly taking his time.

"What's the deal?" yelled Harri. "Are we going down, or what?"

Phil was murmuring to himself and looking confused. "There might be something wrong with the scanner. According to this there's people down there, but no actual signs of life. I'll check the history log."

"I knew this place would be a dive," Davis complained. "Can't we just blow this joint and go to Paganett?"

"That's why," Phil said. "It's a freezing, barren place where people get sent if they don't kiss arse. They're down there but they ain't living any kind of life. Fair enough, we'll just do another lap." With that settled, he set the cruiser off again at lightning speed. "Have another drink and when you're finished, I'll stop."

Kam handed them each a Tequila Slammer. Seeing as they were going to Earth he figured they should sample some of the drinks the planet had to offer. With three swirls of the glass, a bang down on the bar top and a quick tossing back of the liquid they were suddenly wiser about Earth's culture. They reasoned that if this stuff was bottled and sold as a serious drink then the Earth was in more trouble than any rumours on Dectarus had allowed for. Their eyes smarted and their throats burned. Sumo noticed his sinuses had cleared.

"OK, we're done," croaked Tash. "Stop now."

"Where'd that stuff come from?" Harri asked Kam, his face screwed up in disgust.

Kam checked the label on the bottle. "Mexico."

"Make sure we don't go there Phil," called Harri. "My liver's not up to the abuse."

Phil stopped the cruiser. He scanned the area. "We're above New Zealand. There are signs of activity below. Wanna take a look? Hold on, I'm only picking up on some sort of woolly quadruped. That's all that seems to be down there." Phil consulted the all-knowing log. "There are more sheep - which are the woolly things - than people and they're not exactly party animals. Well, I think we should definitely pass on that place. Can't imagine too many things you could do with a sheep. Have another drink and I'll move off again."

Kam handed out a double whiskey. The drink went down smoothly. Phil stopped. "Third time lucky? We're over Adelaide. I'm getting signs of life and it's two-legged this time. History log says it's a small, largely overlooked country town in Australia with two churches and a pub. Population: old people who drive badly."

"Do they have naked women?" Sumo asked.

Phil scanned the information. "It doesn't say."

"Move on then." Sumo wasn't interested in wasting time.

Phil set the cruiser in motion. "Have another drink."

Martini. Not bad, could be wetter. Could be bigger too.

Another pit stop. "Africa. They've …"

"… Naked women?" Sumo interrupted.

"Doesn't … "

"… Move on."

Another drink. "China. It's the most populated …"

"Naked women?"

Phil shrugged.

"Next."

"Relax, big fella, we'll get you some naked women." Marc used the most soothing tone he could muster. If Sumo was allowed to carry on they'd never get down to the planet. "Make this a good one Phil."

Globe circled. Drinks swallowed. All stop.

"OK, we're over London. History: Capital of England. I thought the capital of England was the letter 'E'?" Phil looked genuinely confused and shook his head. He quickly condensed the country's history. "There's a bit about double decker buses, pork pies and a picture of something called a Stonehenge."

"Women?"

"Yes. The place is totally controlled by one."

"Jackpot. A dominatrix!" Sumo whooped in delight.

Phil decided he wouldn't show Sumo the picture of the Queen. It was better to let him fantasise about whips and leather. It helped keep him settled.

"Hey Harri, check this out. Is that your Grandad's holiday house?"

Harri reeled his way over to the history screen. He stared at Stonehenge, blinking furiously in an effort to focus his vision. No clarity was forthcoming and his eyelids were beginning to ache from overuse. "Maybe," he shrugged, and made his way back to the bar.

It was indeed Grandad's holiday house, of sorts, except Grandad Hubert's retreat was located beach front, next to the pyramids, on Mars. His house and Stonehenge were all that remained of one man's deluded dream. Some long gone ancestor, who had more money than taste, rather pretentiously decided to build the same style home on every planet in the system.

Had his wife not run off with Rockman Rocker, the ugliest, fattest, smelliest bank manager who ever overcharged on accounts, he certainly would have succeeded but bankruptcy saw him leave half built stuff all over the place. Eventually the deserted structures either fell down or slowly got ripped off.

As it was, Stonehenge was but a shadow of its former self and it was still being snaffled, chunk by chunk. One morning it just wouldn't be there anymore and a band of toothless crooks would be living very comfortably on the warm side of Fricshun.

Fortunately for Grandad Hubert, all his relatives before him had maintained the holiday home, mostly because of its location, location, location. Harri would eventually inherit it. Grandma Sheri was already furnishing it for him with all her old, spare stuff from home. She knew her grandson would appreciate the grandmotherly touch of cross-stitch pictures and crocheted blankets should he ever take a girl there.

"Hey guys," Phil called, "I've picked up something flying towards us." He scanned the object then consulted the history log. "It's called an aeroplane. It's like the cruiser 'cept not everyone's got one and it's restricted to the confines of this planet. Here it comes."

The guys knew what to do; they did what all good party animals do - they dropped their pants, spread their butt cheeks, pressed their arses up to the windows of the cruiser and gave two hundred and fifty horrified people a brown eye.

The plane sped on by.

The jet landed at Heathrow. Not one person aboard the plane could begin to comprehend what it was they had seen ten short minutes ago. No one spoke. One woman thought that the aliens, and she knew beyond a doubt they were aliens, had rendered everyone speechless, probably with some sort of sophisticated vocal-chord freezing thought wave, so they wouldn't be able to tell anyone what they'd seen.

She secretly hoped this was the case because, for a price, she would force herself to tell her story of terror in the skies to the right paper or magazine, maybe even get on the telly, depending on who offered her more. She would tell the press how the aliens had been hovering menacingly close to their plane; how the bright round object - or was it sausage shaped? - with all those multicoloured lights, danced around their plane as if it were toying with it, or possibly trying to cause it to crash. Yes, that was good. That's how it was.

And their faces! She'd never forget their faces. Two hideous, puffy cheeks with four welt like protrusions on either side, as if a worm creature living under the skin was waiting to erupt and invade a human body. And one eye, staring cruelly. No nose, no mouth, just an eye. Like a third eye that saw all and knew all. Was Earth a safe place anymore? She didn't think so, not after what she'd just witnessed and, to the most generous bidder, she'd be happy to tell them why.

Chapter 3

The guys felt they had outdone themselves on the amusement scale and they laughed so hard it hurt. They rolled on the floor, clutching their aching sides. Tears streamed from their eyes and when Tash let out an ear piercing machine gun fart the hilarity of it all was too much. Fists hammered the floor and feet kicked the air. The violent expulsion of wind from an anus was always a guaranteed crowd pleaser.

Exhaustion eventually overtook and their laughter slowly dissipated. They moaned and groaned and lay still until the urgent need for a drink gave them the strength to stand up. Tash was last to move. He used Joc as a support post to claw his way to an upright position. His intestines were grabbing and the convulsions that racked his body started a nasty chain of events in his abused stomach. What began as a mild ripple soon became tsunami like in nature. His stomach heaved up to his throat, his cheeks puffed out and Joc caught the 'I'm gonna chuck' expression on his face. Not wanting to get puked on, Joc gave Tash a mighty shove in the general direction of the toilet. Tash hurled his body against the door, dived inside the room and, without having time to take aim, spewed up seventeen different lots of alcohol. The smell made him gag. He chucked again. His body slumped to the floor, relieved.

After a moment of rest, and now feeling like a million bucks, he got to his feet and groped for the light switch. Light flooded the room. Tash brought his hands to his head and groaned. This was most definitely not the toilet and his vomit was most definitely not contained within anything even remotely resembling a toilet. What a hassle. The fact that his chuck was splashed up the walls, amongst other places, ordinarily would have concerned him greatly, well a little at least, until he spotted nine 'Zippy Mowers'.

Tash ran out of the room and up to Phil. "Sorry about puking everywhere but did you know you got Zippy Mowers?"

Phil looked at him. "Whaddya mean you puked everywhere? Did you clean it up?"

"Not yet. The Zippy Mowers - can we use them?" he persisted.

"Zippy Mowers? Where?" Phil didn't know what he was on about.

"Come here and I'll show you. Hey guys, check this out." Tash led them to what was making him highly excitable.

They stood at the door and surveyed the mess. Talk about projectile vomiting. Chunky bits were everywhere.

"Kam, bring a cloth and a bucket of water, would you," yelled Phil. "Tash, you're disgusting."

If the cruiser hadn't been his responsibility, Phil would have found the vomit highly amusing. The trajectory and spread alone were quite a feat, but he couldn't fully appreciate their worth. The other guys patted Tash on the back and congratulated him on a job well done.

"The mowers," Tash said impatiently. "Look at them." He pointed to the back of the room.

Nine brand-spanking-new mowers sat in a line in the far corner of the storage hangar. Phil figured they must have fallen off the back of a passing cargo scowl. No way could his old man afford this lot. Probably got 'Shifty's Tow' to bring this find in too.

Treading carefully, so as to avoid Tash's stinking, steaming mess, they got in for a closer look. The mowers were the latest model available on Yecta. It would be at least a year before Dectarus saw them. Phil's old man obviously planned to be selling them first, and for a very tidy sum too, no doubt. Oh well, business was business. Better you doing the deals than some other guy.

Tash ran a finger over the metal. They were a nice looking unit. "Can we use them?" he asked Phil.

Phil looked a bit unsure. He wouldn't mind having a go. These beauties were supposed to practically fly. He looked at the guys. "I don't know. What if we bust them up? The old man would go viral."

"That's what E.P.'s for," reminded Joc.

That settled it. "OK. I'll find somewhere we can go. But Tash has gotta clean up his guts first. I'll stop when he's done."

Phil grabbed another drink and set the cruiser in motion. He dropped the propulsion mechs down so they were travelling at twelve hundred kp/h, which suited him fine because he didn't wanna be picked up for speeding. At night there were no speed restrictions, but at four-thirty in the afternoon you never knew who was watching.

Everyone left Tash to clean up on his own. He dropped it so he had to mop it.

Tash worked fast. He was itching to have a go on the 'latest trend for easier gardening'. He'd heard you could put a propulsion unit into one of those things and you'd practically got yourself a sports machine. They were hot news and hot property. He threw the rag into the bucket and got up off his knees. "Finished," he yelled.

Phil stopped the cruiser. "OK, we're somewhere called Yorkshire. This is ideal. It's a lot of farm land. Plenty of space to get out and let loose." He brought the cruiser down to about ten feet off the ground. Below them was a huge field filled entirely with a straw like material. He opened the hatch.

After grabbing a six pack of Champion Beer each the guys scrambled to get a mower, falling over each other in their hurry. Harri pushed Sumo out of the way of the red one. Red was his favourite colour and he wanted it. He jumped behind the wheel and started her up. It didn't make a sound. Racing down the hatch and out of the cruiser the mower sailed to the ground, landed with a thud and then raised itself up two inches above the earth. Harri didn't even blink. He was off and running, flattening the tall wheat as he went. Each of the guys followed suit.

With one thud after another they left the cruiser. Harri had gotten up to top speed - 90 kp/h - when he hit a rock. His mower lifted up at the front, tipped to the right and threw him out the side. Marc, who was fast coming up behind, ran straight over him. He didn't even stop. If these mowers had worked on the old blade system Harri would have been a goner. Luckily they worked on the pressure wave system so Harri was fully intact leaving only an impression of his body in the earth. He stood up and looked around to see where his mower had gotten to. It was running along the field following Marc's path.

The others passed him at near top speed, yelling for him to get out of the way. Kam trundled up the rear. Harri jumped onto Kam's mower, shoving him over away from the controls, and set off after his runaway machine. He pushed the mower to the limits, passing Sumo and Joc. Harri loved speed. Kam looked nervous. He wasn't into dangerous stunts anymore.

Catching up to his mower, Harri pulled up alongside. With a mighty leap he left Kam to himself. Landing relatively painlessly in the driver's seat, he put the power back on and joined Marc, Tash, Phil and Davis. They'd lined up side by side and were ready to have a race. The beer made them invincible.

If the guys could have revved their machines, they would have. They waited as Joc and Sumo joined the line-up. The field stretched out ahead of them for miles. Without waiting for Kam, and with a yell to go from Joc, the mowers shot forward. Skimming above the ground the machines fought for first place. Somehow Harri managed to push his that little bit harder. It was the colour; had to be.

Marc and Joc followed on Harri's tail. Nudging closer they bumped the back of the mower. The knock interrupted its motion sensor and it faltered slightly. Marc came in on Harri's right, sideswiped his mower and sent it crashing into Joc's. They spun off course. Beer came out of Joc's nose. Marc assumed the lead.

Davis, Sumo and Tash went after Marc, ignoring Harri and Joc who had tipped over and were trying to get their mowers back upright. They were blaming each other for the accident.

"Losers," yelled Phil as he tried desperately to keep up with the field. He couldn't understand how they were getting away from him because he was pushing the mower as hard as it would go. He gripped the wheel tighter, as if that would somehow make a difference to the speed, and concentrated on going faster. Unfortunately the mower wasn't a mind reader and so maintained its speed. The others had gotten way in front.

Joc and Harri stopped arguing and helped each other get their mowers the right way up. Harri thought about leaving Joc to do his own but decided they should gang up on Marc, who had caused the trouble in the first place. By clicking the start button twice they picked up extra speed and raced straight past Phil, one on either side, scaring the shit out of him when they sandwiched him in for a brief moment.

Kam decided not to race. He'd started to but his nerves got the better of him. He couldn't afford to lose anymore of his brain. Sure, the lab were trying to get funding to put in a few extra bits for him but he couldn't risk going home completely empty headed. He did a few low speed donuts and tried to spell out his name in the field. He watched the others from a safe distance.

Finally Phil caught up to the others, only because they'd stopped racing forward and were now circling around and underneath the cruiser. They started to circle out wide and, to see who could maintain better control, brought the circles in tighter until they couldn't turn anymore.

Because Harri knew no fear, he did a full circle in half the time it took the others. They were too cautious on the curves. Harri just went flat out.

"Phil, so glad you could make it," Marc said.

"There's something wrong with my mower. I couldn't get much out of it."

Joc came up alongside Phil and reached into the front of the mower. "Try this," he said, and did the magic double click.

The mower went into a frenzied spin because Phil was leaning on the wheel. Gathering up some common sense he straightened her up and raced back in the direction he'd just come from. He could hear the others coming up behind.

"First one back to Kam is the winner," Tash yelled as he tried to knock Phil out of the way and take top position.

Flying as hard and fast as they could, Harri got directly in front of Marc and Joc got directly behind. Sumo and Davis decided to join in and got either side of him. Marc was blocked in. He was getting bumped from every angle. Tash and Phil were too intent on being the winner to care about what was going on behind them.

"Crunch time," yelled Joc at the top of his voice, as if he was leading warriors into battle.

Harri slammed on the brakes, Joc sped up and Davis and Sumo turned inwards, all at the exact same moment. The force of the impact sent shock waves through Marc's body. His mower became four inches shorter and three inches thinner. The guys whistled and hollered.

"And again," Joc yelled.

With precision timing, they dealt Marc another blow. Every inch of his body reverberated, inside and out. He bit his tongue. This was getting viral. The mower was reduced in size again. He turned the wheel sharply to the right, trying to push Davis out of the way so he could make a clean break, but Davis didn't budge. Marc knew he had only one option left before the next crunch caved the whole mower in. He didn't wanna lose a leg before the wedding. It would screw up the photos.

He turned to Sumo. "Let me outta here Sumo or I'll tell Sotty about Intoe."

"Don't listen to him Sumo, he won't tell nothin'," Davis said.

Sumo didn't look too sure.

"Don't fall for it. He's desperate," Joc said.

Sumo still didn't look too sure. If his wife found out about what he'd gotten up to on his buck's night, he'd be a goner. Sotty was not a calm woman. She wasn't even stable. She could really hurt him. He'd had a hard enough time explaining how his nuts had shrivelled up. Luckily she knew nothing about sexually transmitted diseases. What to do, what to do?

Marc won. Sumo was more afraid of Sotty than he was of the guys. He steered away and let Marc out. With a triumphant shout Marc raced off. Joc, Davis and Harri let him go. They followed Marc as he headed towards Kam, Tash and Phil.

"Sumo, you're weak," Harri picked as Sumo joined the group. "It's an unwritten code that no one tells anything about what goes on at a buck's party. If wifey-to-be ever found out she'd never marry the sap."

"I don't care," said Sumo. "The house is in Sotty's name and I don't wanna risk losing anything. She's tougher than you guys think."

"We know. We've seen her skin. How'd she get it to look like polished steel? Is that natural?" Davis asked.

Sumo gave Davis a filth look. "I'd like to see you do better. You've never even had a girlfriend. Whattsa matter with you?"

"He's bloody ugly," said Marc.

It was Davis's turn to give the filthy looks.

They could have sat picking for hours but the sun was starting to lose its tiny bit of warmth and they agreed they needed another drink. They'd finished their beers ages ago so they ambled back to the cruiser ready for more liquid sustenance. Before climbing back aboard they all had a much needed leak, turning it into a competition to see who could piss the furthest. Davis was out of the running because he had very little equipment to use. He made a mental note to ring the lab in the morning. They sprayed their alcohol filled urine everywhere. Harri won. He made an arch twelve foot high and sixteen foot long. The guys had never seen anything like it.

"Muscle control," he told them. It was a proud moment. If only they gave out medals for such feats.

They each subtracted five drinks from their total, for ridding their body of toxins.

Phil lowered the hatch all the way to the ground and the guys drove the mowers up. Except for Kam's, they all had dings and dents. E.P. had his work cut out for him. He guaranteed everything would look like new or payment was returned in full and E.P. didn't like giving back his fee.

Settling back down they made ready to head back to the city. Phil set the co-ordinates and the cruiser lifted up. "We'll cruise back slowly so the city'll be pumping when we get there."

"Wait a sec Phil, open the hatch and I'll dump this bucket of chuck otherwise it'll start stinking," said Tash.

Balancing on the side of the opening Tash emptied the bucket in the field. The wind sent the contents flying in all directions. Looking down at the field he started laughing. He put the bucket down and signalled to Phil to lift the hatch.

"Hey guys, look out the windows and tell me what you think our racing strip looks like," he said.

They all got up and looked. Where the mowers had flattened down the wheat, a shape had emerged.

Sumo recognised it first. "It looks like a Phallian's private parts," he said. "Right down to the square bits coming off the sides."

How the Phallians had the cheek to refer to their parts as private was something of a mystery seeing as they walked around with their bits permanently on show - and it was not a pretty sight, especially when the wind blew. Its shape, however, did go a long way to explaining why their children were bloody ugly. Phallus was not a recommended holiday destination for prudes or those who liked to be able to tell the difference between males and females.

Davis was nervous. "You reckon anyone'll notice it there? We couldn't get arrested for making pornographic pictures, could we?" He didn't like trouble; it made him break out in a rash. "They got laws against that on some planets."

Joc looked at him and shook his head. "Who's gonna know it was us, you knobless twit. Besides, it wasn't like we did it on purpose, it just happened to end up that shape. No one'll notice anyway; it's in the middle of nowhere. Don't get barometric over it. Let's go Phil, we got some nightlife awaiting."

Phil set the cruiser in motion, buzzed around the field twice at break neck speed, slowed down, and trundled off back towards the city at a slow three hundred kp/h. He wanted to give the sun a chance to set so when they got there the parties would be starting up.

It was about half an hour after the cruiser had departed that the farmer saw the handy work of the guys. Bringing his pet cow, Bella, back from the outlying pastures of the property to the barn for the night, he noticed a section of the wheat in the field had been mysteriously flattened. And even stranger than that was the fact that it had been flattened into a very distinct, but unusual pattern. On top of that, Bella wouldn't go anywhere near the flattened grain.

What the farmer couldn't detect, but Bella could, was the reek of the piss and vomit that had been thoughtlessly discharged there, along with spilled beer that contained the saliva of the rare and noxious Plenium Bug. Bella was quite simply repulsed by the foul odours wafting up from the field. The farmer thought her reactions were something more significant than that. He just knew, or rather hoped, something unnatural had occurred here. Should he call the police or the newspaper first? He'd have to think on that one.

Walking around the largest circle, the farmer looked for clues as to who or what could have done such a thing to his crop. He clearly knew it hadn't been there this morning. You couldn't miss something as long and as wide as this. When he'd gone in for his lunch it hadn't been there either. He could only figure that it had happened when he was having his afternoon nap. That would explain why he'd not seen or heard anything. Whoever, or whatever, did this, he concluded, was not of this world. There was definitely a story, and a few quid, in that theory. He'd call the paper first.

Chapter 4

Racing the mowers had hyped the guys up and they were all talking over top of each other, bragging about their superior driving skills and being generally delusional about their abilities. Joc, however, was sitting quietly. Just a little too quietly for Marc's liking. He knew he should start getting nervous. And Marc didn't like the way Joc was looking at him either, but rather than ask what his problem was and risk giving him any excuse to be a bastard he strolled to the bar, grabbed the smallest drink and knocked it back. Bad move. It was a Gingy Hot-Beet, a drink that needed to be sipped and not downed in one go.

Marc gasped for breath and his eyes watered. Drinking one of those was like drinking pure fire. It seemed to suck all the oxygen from your lungs. Kam quickly handed him a White Wine Cooler. A cheap and nasty drink by all accounts but short of giving him water, which was a definite no-no, it was the only drink capable of cooling Marc's insides and getting some air back into his chest.

Marc coughed and spluttered. All eyes turned to him and he felt very uncomfortable.

"You seem a bit tense there, Marc," Joc said rather smugly. "Guys, don't you think he looks tense?"

They agreed.

"You need to relax; kick back; put your feet up," Joc continued, smiling a bit too broadly. He glanced at Sumo and Harri and gave a slight nod. They stood up and walked towards the storage hangar.

Marc didn't like the look of that, not one little bit. They'd obviously planned something cruel and sadistic. He looked at Joc, his eyes pleading for mercy. No effect. He started to protest; that Jendee would kill him if he went home with anything missing or worse, with anything added to his body. As if the guys cared. All they cared about was having a good time at his expense. Really, he shouldn't have been surprised. He'd done it to Sumo and one or two others over the years. He began to wish he'd stayed home and gone out with his folks.

Harri and Sumo were coming towards him, pushing a chair that was on castors. Oh no, 'Portable Torture'. This was bad. Very bad. If he tried to duck and weave Sumo would pin him down and he knew that if he got a whiff of Sumo's armpit he wouldn't live to see his wedding day. The guy stank in an unnatural way. Even on the coldest days he had chronic B.O. So, Marc reasoned, should he risk death by suffocation or, at the very least, come away with only brain damage or should he just go along with the game and hope they didn't hurt him too much?

Before he had a chance to choose, they were on him. Joc pinned his arms behind his back and Harri kicked the back of his knees so he was forced to sit down. Davis wrapped rope around his wrists and ankles so he couldn't escape. Marc was helpless. He decided to struggle and scream until Sumo sat on him. After that he barely breathed.

"Hairy things," Sumo said, holding out his hand.

From out of his shirt pocket Phil produced two fat, furry caterpillars that he'd picked up at the field.

Marc knew what was coming. "Don't," he begged. "Come on guys, please."

Phil held Marc's head steady as Sumo ran a line of glue along the bottom of each larvae and stuck them over Marc's eyes. He now had two very hairy and obvious eyebrows. There goes the wedding photos, he thought. Fortunately for the caterpillars they'd both died from shock when Phil had shoved them in his pocket. They never would have adapted to life on Marc.

"Speaking from experience," Sumo said, "the glue'll break down in about two weeks if you don't try to remove it sooner, otherwise you can double that time frame. It's very resilient. And don't try to pull the creatures off 'cos half your face'll come with 'em."

Marc really wished he'd stayed home. Whose stupid idea was it to torture some poor idiot just because he was getting married? Like the guy needed the extra aggravation. Maybe it was designed so that marriage looked easy after this. Marc hoped so. He began to wish he'd been kinder to Sumo then maybe he would have had one ally, but he hadn't been kind. He'd been a total and utter bastard. Still, that didn't give anyone the right to be mean to him.

"Get off me you stench fiend," Marc yelled at Sumo. "You're killing me. Kam, a drink please. Wait, better make that two."

Kam delivered and was kind enough to hold them for Marc while he drank. He needed some quick numbing, even though Sumo had managed to block the flow of blood to the lower part of his body.

"More. Get me two more."

"That's the spirit butt-boy. Drink up." Joc turned to Phil. "Where are we now?"

Phil checked the map. "We're near London, travelling over the motorway. It's a long road that cars speed on."

"Perfect," said Joc.

Taking another piece of rope out of the storage hangar, Joc tied it around Marc and the chair so they were tightly bound together, leaving a length of about one hundred and fifty feet available.

"Phil, come down to about ten feet off the ground and open the hatch," requested Joc.

"Whaddaya gonna do to me you impotent knob jockey?" Marc's voice was understandably filled with panic.

Joc ignored him.

"OK," Phil called, "we're nearly there. I just gotta let this lot of cars go before I go much lower. Traffic's pretty light. We should have a fairly clear run for a bit."

The guys pushed the chair over to the hatch door. Joc tied the loose end of the rope to the handle of the emergency escape pod.

"That looks pretty secure," Tash said.

"How's the traffic Phil?" Joc asked.

"All clear. I'm releasing the hatch now."

"You ready Marc? Anything you wanna kiss good-bye before you go, like your nuts?" Joc was having the time of his life.

"You'll pay for this Joc. Believe me." Marc knew they were empty words. The road below looked hard and uninviting.

"Guys, grab the chair and on three we'll push. OK, a one, ana two, ana three - push!"

They thrust the chair forward. It rolled with tremendous speed down the hatch, flew through the air for about eight seconds and dropped to the road in a tooth crunching thud. Miraculously it stayed upright. It sped along the motorway.

"Lift 'er up Phil and put the light on him. I wanna see his face," Joc said.

The cruiser inched up until the slack on the rope was taken up and Marc was underneath them. The light shone on him, illuminating half the motorway in the process. Phil would have to tell his old man what a great job the light did. Putting a bit more power on, the cruiser dragged Marc along at two hundred kp/h. His screams were carried off with the wind, which was bloody cold.

The chair twisted and turned and balanced unevenly. All the three-sixties it was doing was making Marc dizzy and sick. He was sure he was going to go over at any moment. The last four drinks he'd had in quick succession were not happy about the situation either. Marc tried to look up and yell to the guys to stop but the light was blinding him and he couldn't keep his thoughts together long enough to get anything out of his mouth other than 'aaaaahhh'.

Marc passed a couple of cars that were going considerably slower than he was. Phil was manoeuvring the cruiser beautifully so Marc weaved around them, never getting closer than six feet to any part of the vehicles. He screamed for help as he whizzed by their windows. Not one person looked at him. Not one person attempted to help.

It was a quiet night on the motorway, which was just as well, under the circumstances. The few drivers who shared the road with Marc could see him coming for miles. Too frightened to look at where the light was coming from and figure out how this man was managing to do speeds in excess of theirs in only an old office chair, they stared straight ahead. The drivers could hear a faint scream as Marc rolled past. Best not to get involved, they thought. It could be some sort of initiation ceremony or, worse still, a revival of 'Beadle's About'.

A lot of night clubbing Brits, who might normally have gone to London for the evening, were heading to Yorkshire instead to see, first hand, a mysterious crop circle that had appeared out of the blue. An old farmer and his cow had made the six o'clock news. The farmer's wife was offering bed and breakfast, cheap, with tours of the circle for a tiny bit extra. A photo cost five pound more, seven if you wanted the farmer and the cow.

In a possibly related story on the same bulletin, a woman with a bad hairdo and a hoarse voice told of a terrifying encounter with hideous aliens terrorising the plane she was on. Whilst she didn't offer much comment on the ordeal, due to the exclusive rights of her story being sold to a woman's magazine, she did talk of the trauma she'd suffered in the hours since the experience. She surmised she'd probably never get a decent night's sleep again. The other passengers and crew declined to comment, refusing to give in to histrionics whilst considering the possibility the aeroplane food had somehow brought on a mass hallucination. It had been known to happen.

Chapter 5

Marc's wild ride continued.

"Go faster Phil," Sumo called. "He's not screaming hard enough yet."

"Hang on, I'm picking up on some sort of electronic device. It's straight ahead, about thirty k's away. I'll see if the computer knows what it is." Phil read from the screen, "It's called a radar unit. The police use it to extract money from people's wallets. We're OK then, we haven't got either." He sped up.

Marc didn't know where he was anymore. He rather fancied he was at home, tripping out on some new and illegal drug. He thanked his mother and father for having him and the Members of the Association who had voted him 'Fornicator Of The Year'. Delirium could be a good thing - it allowed for a rich fantasy life.

"I'm gonna turn the light off as we get closer to the cops," said Phil. "It's probably better if we sneak by. I don't wanna be done for drunk flying."

Coming fast around the curve in the road the chair swung out wide and lifted into the air. Marc collected a branch from a tree complete with an angry looking owl. The owl reminded Marc of an exchange student from Delta Rewden who'd stayed with his family for a school term.

"How you doin' Mincko. Long time, no see."

The chair landed back down on the road, skidded sideways and nearly toppled over but corrected itself just in time. The owl flew away wondering how people had survived for so long with so few brains and even less sense. How rude, thought Marc, he could have said hello.

They were five clicks away from the police so Phil killed the light. He pushed the cruiser up to two hundred and eighty kp/h. They'd be on them in a minute. The wheels on the chair were wearing down so the ride was getting rougher. Marc's head was swimming.

Around the curve the chair raced past the police and their radar unit. Either the cruiser's speedo was slightly off or the radar was because Marc clocked in at doing two hundred and ninety-two kp/h; his vomit - travelling backwards - at two hundred and ten. Wind drag must have slowed it down.

Marc wore a lot of it. His shirt was sticking to his chest and he had lumps of something in his caterpillars, up his nose and in his hair. He tried to think what he'd eaten that was thick and sticky. Nothing came to mind. Initially the vomit had been warm but it cooled down quickly in the cold English air. This was Jendee's fault. If she hadn't asked him to marry her he wouldn't be in this mess. Marc really wanted to lie down and die but he knew those bastards wouldn't let him. He wasn't even sure they were ever going to let him back into the cruiser. They'd have to show mercy soon.

Sitting out in the cold on a Saturday night when everybody else was drinking and having fun had made the coppers mean. A permanent scowl was etched into their features. They'd gotten assigned traffic duty a year ago after they'd been caught nicking a packet of jelly tots from the faulty snack machine. Their excuse of sugar withdrawal was not accepted and they'd been made an example of. Rain, hail, snow, Arctic winds, excessive heat - it didn't matter, they were always there. Every night, every week, every month.

Traffic into London was unusually slow for a Saturday. In the three hours they'd been on they'd booked one vicar and one smart-mouthed woman who was a left over from the long dead punk era. And that was it. Where was everybody? The coppers didn't like freezing for nothing. The next person they caught would really get a serve. All they needed was a hundred more pinches and they'd be back to their old, more comfortable, non-traffic duty beat. Deliverance wasn't long off.

Staring at the digital display read-out on the unit, the younger copper was thinking about that nice lady he'd met last week at the supermarket. She really knew a lot about melons and rice crackers. He considered those two of the more important qualities to look for in a woman. The older copper was complaining about the weak tea his missus had given him again. It was too milky and she must have waved the tea bag in front of the pot instead of putting it in. Tomorrow night she'd better get it right or he was going to give her a speeding ticket. He might give her mother one too, just for the hell of it. The fact that the old biddy didn't even drive was largely beside the point at this moment in time.

After quite a lull in the traffic the display suddenly sprang into life. The numbers rolled around over each other to rest at an amazing two hundred and ninety-two kilometres per hour. Someone was in one hell of a mighty hurry. This was worth the equivalent of ten tickets at least. Before they had a chance to gloat about their good fortune, from around the curve came what looked like a man on a chair. As quickly as he appeared he virtually disappeared, down the road. Gone. Just like that, gone. They couldn't even get the licence plate number, because there wasn't one. What on God's green earth was that thing? And then they were hit by something that registered at a speed lesser than that of the chair.

They looked at each other. The old copper got the torch and shone it on the younger copper's face. He was covered in some sort of liquid.

They both were. Because traffic duty can do strange things to a man's mind after a while, they were afraid they'd been the victims of sabotage - by what they couldn't fathom. But because any attempt to remove the sticky liquid might activate some sort of flesh-eating reaction they sat perfectly still, too scared to move. Whatever it was that had hit them stunk to high heaven, that much they did know.

Twenty-nine speeding motorists went unpunished as they sat there until their shift was over, speaking only when necessary, which wasn't often, and barely moving a muscle. There had been no noticeable changes to either man's skin, but six hours wasn't a long time in the life of a germ as far as they were concerned. Slowly they packed up the radar, gently got into the car and drove back to the station. They decided they'd see the doctor before they went home. Just in case.

Chapter 6

Phil put the light back on Marc. He was doing a good job of staying upright. Well, the chair was. Marc's head was slumped forward and his body looked loose and limp. Phil hoped they hadn't killed him. Jendee would not be pleased.

"I think we'd better haul him up. He's not looking too good," Phil kindly suggested. "He's not even screaming anymore."

Slowing to a full stop Phil lowered the cruiser down to five feet off the road. The guys grabbed the rope and pulled Marc back on board. Lifting him up to the hatch was hard work. The chair was tipping in all directions. Finally the wheels made contact with the metal. Phil closed the hatch and raised up just in time to avoid a collision with a lorry that was carrying frozen peas to London.

The lorry driver could see it. A shiny metal object with flashing disco lights of all colours. Of course it wasn't real. It was the caffeine and the tablets messing with his mind. He didn't attempt to slow down or stop because nothing was really there. Why should he be late getting to the depot because a guy was being abducted by aliens? It wasn't any of his business. There was no business, because it wasn't there.

And then what wasn't there was suddenly gone. He knew it hadn't been real. He wasn't losing his marbles at all. He was just a guy doing a job that required you to drive on your wits, a couple of hours sleep and a pot of coffee every hour. No problem. A mirage; a figment of his imagination; a delusion. He could handle that.

He checked his watch. Time for another pill. He popped it happily and carried on singing old country tunes to the pixie he'd picked up in Cambridge.

Back on board the cruiser the guys gathered around Marc. He sat there perfectly motionless. He'd looked better, that's for sure. Proudly they realised they'd achieved one of their objectives - he'd puked on himself. The party wasn't a total loss.

They untied him. Without the rope holding him up he fell sideways and crashed onto the floor. He lay frozen at their feet.

"Is he alive?" Davis asked. He was ready to bail out at the first sign of trouble.

Joc nudged Marc's motionless body with his foot. "He's faking, I reckon."

"I dunno," said Tash, "it looks like rigors has set in."

"Don't get carried away," said Joc, "I've seen this before. Sumo - armpit."

As Sumo started to kneel down, Marc opened his eyes, sat bolt upright and leapt to his feet. He'd tried to stay still but he couldn't control his survival instincts.

"Told you he was faking it," Joc said with a self-satisfied smile.

Marc had gotten up too quickly. His head was thumping and his stomach was churning. He opened his mouth to say something but all that came out was another wave of booze and unrecognisable food. He felt a little better, especially seeing as Joc wore some of it on his shoes and it was puke number two. One more, he thought, and he wouldn't be subjected to the 'Buck's Special'. The mercy rule was every buck's friend.

Joc's face took on a disgusted expression as he shook his feet to get the vomit off. "Thanks a lot. These shoes were new."

"Boo hoo. Anyway, it's your fault. You told Sumo to do the armpit thing, so you deserve it," Marc said, wiping his mouth. He turned to Sumo. "You gotta do something about your sweat glands, you're a deadly weapon. I don't know how you and Sotty can stand it."

"We had our foul odour senses removed."

"Well the rest of us aren't so lucky." Marc looked at Joc. "I can't wait for the day you get married. And don't think you won't, because you will. You are going to get absolutely hammered on your Buck's Night."

Joc yawned. "Yeah, I'm sure I'll be begging for mercy."

Screw you, bastard. "Well, I'm up for another drink," Marc said as he started to wander over to the bar. His colour was returning and he needed to kill the disgusting taste in his mouth

"Not so fast," said Phil, "clean up your chuck first."

Damn, he was hoping to get out of it. "Kam, bucket please." Kam dutifully brought the bucket over and handed it to Marc.

It was a pity Kam wasn't too bright because he was actually the best looking, the best dressed and the least vulgar and crude of all the guys. The others knew women went for that kind of thing so, to better their chances of meeting some, they had him hang around them. It was after his accident at the seaside resort of Sandd Gritt on Tylamar, where chunks of his brain had been devoured by the much dreaded, yet strangely revered, Mind-Sucker Octobow, that Kam fell victim to being the lackey. That's not to say he'd been exceptionally bright before the accident, he was just not as slow or as docile. The guys preferred him this way.

Marc crawled around on his knees scooping up his mess. This was the worst thing about chucking. If they'd been in a nightclub he would have just left it on the floor for some poor drinks waiter or glass collector to clean up.

Harri had done that once at the Dent room on Battern, a place they were no longer welcome because a Nampereon woman had slipped on it and broken one of her necks, specifically the right one which served her ability to sit for hours in the studio audience of talk shows laughing, clapping and ooohing on cue at anything the host, hostess or guests said. Foot stomping was reserved for the emotive words of another audience member. Luckily that function came from the left neck so her life wasn't totally over.

Anyway, to cut a long story short, she sued the owner, Dentford, for near total loss of enjoyment and purpose in life. The judge awarded her lifetime tickets to all the talk shows, including being a guest on each of them, and seventeen zupion molzars. A fortune by Battern's standards but in Earth's terms it was roughly equal to one hundred and eighty-two pesos with which she could have bought a taco and a small handgun, with the right connections.

Dentford declared bankruptcy, because his insurance company didn't cover acts of gross excreta, and he went into hiding somewhere in the Matsia Nebula. Needless to say, the guys weren't welcome back when new owners took over.

When Marc was finished he decided to take a quick shower and wash his clothes at the same time. He'd wear one of the protection suits he'd seen hanging up whilst his own dried. No problem.

"Be prepared for the consequences if you have a shower, limp boy," Joc threatened, as Marc headed for the bathroom. "You're not supposed to powder your arse every time it gets dirty. There's a penalty for excessive cleanliness."

Marc didn't care what Joc said. Nothing could be worse than what they'd done to him. Besides, he was still cold. He lathered his body and warbled a tune he'd heard E.P. do on karaoke night at the Stardust. E.P. wasn't much of a mover but his voice was good, when it wasn't croaking.

Marc felt as good as new now he'd cleaned himself up. He'd have to do some serious drinking to catch up to the drunken level of the others. This he could do well. Putting the suit on he left the bathroom, hung his wet clothes up and made a bee-line for the bar. Marc shook his head when he heard the inane conversation taking place. The guys were arguing about whether or not the hostess on the game show 'Circle of Destiny' was real or just a store mannequin the producers had wired up to walk, talk and smile at the most basic of levels. Plastic dummy was winning and Sumo was getting huffy because he had the hots for the "ever lovely, Miss Sparkle." Actually, Sumo had the hots for every woman except his own wife. But that was the nature of marriage so you couldn't really blame the guy.

Marc interrupted their argument. "Is this what you're gonna tell people you did on a buck's night? 'Oh yeah, it was great. We sat around talking crap'. Where's your self-respect?" He addressed Phil. "You wanna check where we are?"

Phil obliged. "We're over Piccadilly Circus."

"I hate circuses," Tash said.

"What time is it?" Joc asked.

"It's coming up for eight o'clock."

Marc went to a window and peered out. It was too dark to see anything other than a sprinkling of lights. "You wanna hang around or go somewhere else?"

Everyone looked at each other, none of them willing to make a decision.

Finally Marc made it for them. "Let's get outta here. I think we've seen enough of England for one trip."

"OK." agreed Phil, "We'd probably never get a park anyway."

Phil sat at the controls ready to move off and explore yet another of the places the Earth had to offer. To save going through what they had earlier he set the co-ordinates for: 'anywhere that's got parking, people and pubs' and flicked on the auto-pilot. In a flash they rose to forty thousand feet and the cruiser's navigational computer did its thing.

Marc stood at the bar with a drink in each hand and another three at the ready. He took a mouthful from four of the glasses in succession and felt the fight for supremacy going on his stomach. Each drink was volatile in nature. If he'd taken a mouthful of Hemmy with a mouthful of Grafew, for example, he would have spontaneously combusted, but taking the Hemmy with the Frilip, Bunthion and Jadas only caused a mild stirring of discomfort with the Jadas sucking the alcohol content from the other three and so becoming ten times as potent as it originally was. Once the Jadas had won its battle, usually denoted by a burp that smelt so bad your nose hairs curled, the Grafew could be safely knocked back.

This method of drinking helped to achieve a quick state of inebriation complete with blood shot eyes, obnoxiousness and spitting when talking unnecessarily loud and long about stuff no one was the least bit interested in.

Many a drinker using this method had been known to corner an unsuspecting sober person, pin them against a wall with their arms over the innocent's shoulders, thereby blocking their body in with no means of escape, and slurring incoherently about the trouble with people today or why the migration of the Heely bird was a joyous occasion that should be recognised with a public holiday.

After four hours of non-stop talking and ignoring the fact that their victim was either dead - usually brought about by their own hand, slumped on the floor in a coma or gibbering senselessly about the virtues of sinusitis, the drinker would suddenly need to go to the toilet and, just like that, they'd leave. Their bladder acted as a mercy gauge, eventually. Thankfully, the drinker would never return to the same person twice. Why this was so, was unknown. Money had been put aside for research at one time but unfortunately data collectors had all died, gone mad or mysteriously disappeared.

But regardless of the danger to others in drinking in this way, Marc continued. He was feeling good and he was feeling mellow. He was warm inside and out and he suddenly felt he had a lot to say; important stuff about lawn seed and hairdressers. His head was full of wondrous revelations that he had an overwhelming urge to share.

He could hear the guys talking but his vocal chords were primed to speak at any level greater than the existing noise in the room, including the distorted row coming from a stereo at full volume or a baby's crying. He turned unsteadily to face them, his eyes scanning for the soberest one of the lot.

As bad luck would have it all the guys were passed the 'not drunk enough yet that I risk being rendered brain dead by a crashing bore' stage. Oh well, Marc would just have to enthral them all. Taking centre stage he opened his mouth to speak.

"Did you know…" he started. He thought his voice had come out in a whisper so he upped the volume and projection. "Did you know that with the properties of the Kester Seed being the way they are - which I'll tell you about in a moment - if you swallow one, followed by a hand full of dirt, a patch of grass will grow in your stomach and eventually come out of your head. No, don't protest, it's true. This person told me that because you can't mow it, it just gets out of control and before you know it…"

"What the…" Joc tried to talk over top of him. "Shut up," he yelled.

"… you've got an area ideal for endangered species. Of course you need …"

"Shut up," they all yelled.

"Somebody do something," begged Tash, "he's making my ears bleed."

"… a conservationist to oversee the running of the place. Picnics are usually not…"

"I'll take care of it." Sumo walked over to Marc. His ears were ringing from the noise. He grabbed him by the shoulders and shook him violently. Nothing. Marc continued on.

"… recommended because of the ants but, with a little forward planning, a playground for the kiddies …"

Sumo lifted his arm and pressed his pit to Marc's nose. Still no change. This was not a good sign. Sumo backed away. He'd done all he could.

"… could quite successfully be built. Of course you would need to get …"

Joc suddenly looked hopeful. "Load up a tube of Over-Wham with a Drizon Boost," he yelled to Kam.

Kam didn't hear him.

"… council approval, but with a few zintas placed in the right pocket you …"

Joc would have to load the tube himself. He rushed to the bar and mixed up the only known antidote for Marc's condition. Only in extreme desperate measures was its use advised as the cure could be worse than the symptoms and it could only be used when the offender was torturing more than three people at any one time.

"… can get them to agree to just about anything. I know of a… Ouch."

Joc jabbed the thick needle into Marc and forced the fluid through. Normally the drink was injected into the bum but Marc had the impenetrable protection suit on and so the only available space was his neck. It had to be injected swiftly and as painfully as possible. These rules were only made up because of the agonising tirade the victims had had to endure. It was just a small way of exacting revenge. It had been found that trying to coax or force the person to take the drink orally didn't work because they didn't shut up long enough to swallow.

It went quiet. Blissfully, peacefully quiet. It had worked. And even better, Marc was still standing. Admittedly he looked like a statue, but that was no cause for alarm. At least the guys thought it wasn't. Joc had heard that one guy who'd had the injection had immediately picked up the family cat, plonked himself in an armchair and sat there stroking the cat's fur backwards for two whole weeks. He didn't speak or eat in all that time. The cat died after four days, due to mass irritation, but no one noticed until the guy got up and the cat didn't.

A full minute passed before Marc snapped to. First movement came from his hands which he waved in front of his nose. He screwed up his face and gagged. "Did something die in here? Man, that's putrid." Marc moved, trying to get away from the smell. "Why are you all looking at me like that?" He brought his hand to his neck and rubbed the spot where the needle had gone in. Realisation of what must have occurred suddenly hit him. "Did I start going on about seeds and lawn?"

"Yep," they said.

"Was it painful?"

"Yep."

"Good. Kam, fix me a Poison Rocket."

Kam handed Marc his drink. He served it in a glass the size of a small fish bowl. Marc drank thirstily. Dehydration was a side-effect of the jab. That suited Marc just fine. He intended to break Harri's record of one hundred and twenty-one different drinks consumed in a ten hour period. The six-pack of beer in Yorkshire counted as only one big drink because it was all the same.

For Marc, or any of them, to take the crown they needed to be conscious for five minutes after the last drop had gone down. Harri had made four minutes and eleven seconds. Nevertheless, he was still the record holder. Actually, they were all on their way to reaching personal bests, but because Marc and Tash had thrown up they had to restart their tally from zero. Tash's count was climbing quickly but Marc needed to catch up in a hurry and he was raring to go.

With Marc creating a nuisance the guys hadn't noticed that the cruiser had stopped. Daylight came through the windows.

"How long have we been stopped?" Sumo asked.

"I'll check." Phil went up front. "Only three minutes."

"Why is it light outside?" Joc asked.

"It's four in the afternoon. We're over New York City."

"I've heard of this place," said Davis. "If you breathe the air down there you risk losing a lung."

"Well how do the people live?" asked Sumo

"They walk quickly, never engage in conversation in the street and travel underground. Most of them have built up enough of an immunity to cope day to day as long as they spend most of it indoors, but they can't laugh 'cos it requires you to suck in too much air."

"How do you know all this?" Marc asked.

"I saw it on a science program. Fenny what's-his-face came down here and did a show on the risks of pollution. He concluded that it makes people suspicious and tense."

Phil read from the history log. "There's a Central Park - well we got parking then; there's about eight million people - there's our other requisite, and they got pubs, or bars as they're called here, where people go to avoid peak-hour crush and cab drivers and the main language spoken is an unnatural and aberrant corruption of English. We can handle that."

"But it's day time. We want nightclubs," Marc pouted.

"OK, we'll do a time adjustment jump. We won't lose any of the time we've got left to party but it'll speed up the city's time so it's night. How's around midnight sound?"

"Suits us."

"Right, I'll look up how to do it. I'll find the central parking place first so we can land when it's done."

The cruiser moved off from over Greenwich Village and hovered above Central Park. Phil took in the sight. "Who puts trees in a vehicle park? These people must be nuts. If I hit something I'm gonna deny I got insurance. Just let them try and find me. I'll tell them I'm Nampereon and that'll make them think twice about …"

"… You quite finished?" Joc interrupted. "Hurry up. None of us are getting any younger."

"Sorry, I got carried away. Right… " Phil started mumbling to himself, " … here's what we do for this time jump. I set the warp clock for midnight and then I jump to the left and push that button and then I step to the right and flick that switch and then…" His voice trailed off. He stood at the console with his hands on his hips. Why hadn't it worked? "Oh, I do it again and then… OK, check it out guys, it worked."

Sure enough, it was dark outside and they hadn't felt a thing although there were empty glasses on the bar that hadn't been there before. Phil turned the underneath light on, to make parking easier, and lowered the cruiser down.

"Don't forget to turn your telepathy switches on before we get out," reminded Joc.

Reclining on the roof of his shared apartment in the Village, for which he and five others paid an over-inflated rent to a landlord with a flaky skin complaint and knobby knees, Donny was daydreaming about being a Broadway star. He looked better in a dress than anyone he knew so he couldn't understand why he wasn't the toast of the town. What he failed to see in himself was his total inability to act, sing and dance. Having good legs was just not good enough. No one ever told him this though, they simply took his money for lesson after lesson of all things arty. Where there was a buck to be made in this town, people were making it. He was beginning to think he should have stuck to aromatherapy.

Practising the only line he had in an upcoming very off-Broadway production entitled 'Rappin' in the Rain', he became aware that a shadow had fallen across his face. Opening his eyes lazily, expecting to see a roomy, he couldn't believe what he saw. Above him, directly above him mind you, was a space ship; a UFO - in broad daylight, yet!

He pinched himself to do a reality check. Yes it hurt and yes he was awake. His heart started pounding. What if they abducted him and probed all his orifices and then, when they were done violating him, dumped his naked body in somewhere awful like Tennessee? He knew what happened. He'd seen the X-Files. Too frightened to make any sudden moves in case he drew unwanted attention to himself, he lay there frozen. If he could have acted the types of emotions he was feeling right now he would have been a star a long time ago.

Having time to observe the craft at great length - he was even too scared to blink - he was intrigued by its shape. Contrary to popular myth it was neither disc nor sausage shaped. It looked just like a Caddy and it looked to be very well preserved. It wasn't often you saw such a well cared for vehicle. Rust and dents were commonplace and to its credit it wasn't blowing any smoke either. The owner was obviously a car lover.

If he'd seen the tear made by the rock earlier all his illusions would have been shattered. He couldn't stand imperfection. It caused agitation and turmoil in his already fragile mind. His analyst blamed his mother for the problem. His agent blamed his father. Donny blamed his analyst and his agent.

Thinking that he was definitely going out of his mind for real this time because he was caught up in marvelling at the aesthetics of the craft, he switched his thoughts to reciting the personal mantra his yogi had given him. It was supposed to calm him down and bring him peace. It wasn't working. All he could focus on was being a potential lab rat for several sets of fingers and sharp, shiny instruments.

Before his head could torment him further, the craft moved off.

It didn't blast off at the speed of light nor did it disappear into thin air, it just trundled off as casual as you like. There had been no contact, no abduction, no mind meld, no probing. Oddly, he was a bit disappointed.

Standing up, he walked inside and dialled his agent.

"I've been practising my line," he said. "How does this sound - 'Was that a gunshot I just heard?'"

His agent told him to emphasise the word 'I' and to emote, emote - that was the key.

"By the way," Donny said, "I've just seen a UFO."

His agent advised him to call his analyst and then the 'National Enquirer'. Never miss an opportunity to get in the paper, he said. Good idea, thought Daniel. Any publicity was good publicity.

Chapter 7

Phil had managed to conceal the cruiser behind a group of trees. He decided to hide it because he wasn't sure about parking time restrictions. Recently, when he'd been doing some shopping on Oppen, he'd parked in a two hour zone. He came out of the complex just in time to see the cruiser being towed. The towing company people obviously hung around counting off the seconds because he'd been away only five minutes longer than the allocated time. He chased the tow truck, screaming for the driver to stop, but of course he wouldn't.

It took a note from his mother excusing his inconsiderate behaviour and four bottles of Kouzak to get the thing back. The towing company were having their usual 'one hundred successful tows' celebration party and they needed to top up the bar. Incredibly, they always made sure to tow that exact number every day.

After a smooth and easy landing the guys were ready to go. Marc wondered if he should change out of the protection suit or leave it on because, actually, it looked quite good. Really, his clothes weren't dry enough yet to put back on anyway, so the suit it was. He hoped he wouldn't stand out too much.

It was decided they should head in a southerly direction for no particular reason other than Sumo staggered that way the moment he left the cruiser and, now that he was on his way, there would be no stopping him or changing his direction. He was up to eighty-seven drinks in total and he led the main field by only four drinks. Tash was clawing his way back up quickly - he was on a total of sixty-nine drinks. Marc had done his best in the last half hour to bring his total to forty-four. It had been easy up to about drink thirty-five but then he was forced to slow down because his stomach was bloated and feeling uncomfortable. Kam hadn't had a single drink in the last hour. He'd stopped when he could no longer see out of his left eye. He didn't realise he'd closed the lid when he started seeing double and that nothing was actually wrong with his eye. The guys excused him because he'd put in a good starting effort and they allowed him some leeway because of his partly empty head.

Walking through Central Park was quite pleasant. The air was reasonably clean and odour free. That probably helped to explain why so many people hung around there after dark, but they all seemed a bit odd. The pollution must have affected them when they were young because their eyes darted about wildly and suspiciously as the guys passed them. None of them looked to be very relaxed and trying to pick up on thoughts was a futile exercise because none of them seemed to have any.

Even odder than that, according to the history log, cabs were as necessary an evil as pastrami and tall buildings in the city, yet there didn't seem to be any about. Come to think about it there were no other vehicles parked at all. Suddenly it occurred to Phil that the vehicle park was actually closed for the night. Not that it really mattered to the guys, it wasn't like they had to drive out of there. Nevertheless, Phil was really glad he'd hidden the cruiser. Most of the people they encountered looked like they couldn't be trusted and the last thing he wanted was for the thing to be ripped off and sold for spare parts in some cheap and seedy bar. It was all right for his old man to do stuff like that because when it was other people's things, who cared?

Joc stopped dead in his tracks. He fiddled with his telepathy switch.

"Can you guys hear that?" he asked. "I'm picking up that someone is watching us and thinks we're easy targets for mugging."

Davis didn't like the 'easy targets' inference. "Which direction is it coming from?" he asked. When he got nervous he couldn't use his telepathy to its full advantage.

"It's to the left of this path we're on. The person must be close 'cos I can read their thoughts quite clearly. Are you guys getting it?"

"What's mugging?" Sumo asked. He was messing with his switch because all he was getting was a radio station playing a song about a man claiming that the night was a lonely ol' one. How he was picking it up he didn't know but it was a catchy tune so he didn't mind.

"The history log mentioned mugging as a favourite pastime, like baseball and football. It can be done as either a solo or team event. People beat up on you just for the sport or, if it's their profession, for money, watches and shoes," Phil informed them.

"Well it won't really matter if we do get mugged," said Marc, "we got nothing to steal."

"That's beside the point," said Davis, "you know I can't stand getting hurt." His eyes moved quickly from side to side. To look at him you would have thought he was a long time resident of the city.

"Don't panic," said Harri. "It sounds like there's only two of them. There's seven of us."

"Eight," corrected Tash.

"No, seven. Davis doesn't count."

The guys laughed but instead of being offended Davis was happy to be left out. Kam handed them each a can of Potgut beer from the small knapsack he was carrying.

The muggers leapt out onto the path in front of the guys. At first they were hard to see because their faces were painted green and black and they wore black clothes and hats. The guys smelt them before they saw them.

"Give us your drinks an' give us your fuckin' money now," said the bigger of the two, threatening them with a knife.

Addressing the would-be attackers Harri said, "We haven't got any money but if we did I'd give it to you if you promised to buy some soap. You stink. D'ya ever shower?"

"Who gives a fuck about our bathing habits, give us your fuckin' money." He was edgy as it was. This mugging game was giving him high blood pressure. He'd have to retire before his heart blew up in his chest. And wasn't there anyone left who was afraid of muggers? That was the trouble with this city, no one respected you anymore and people had gotten hard. Instead of doing what they were told they fought back. His job was getting more difficult all the time. It was the media's fault with their anti-crime wave bullshit; stand up for yourself crap; don't be a victim garbage. It just made it tougher for crooks to make a dishonest living.

Yeah well, he thought, fuck these guys, he was gonna carve his name in their guts when he was finished robbing them and leave their bodies where they could be seen by the other gangs. He was owed some respect and maybe he'd get back some of the territory he'd lost.

"Herbie," Joc said sweetly, "you can't even spell so how you gonna carve your name anywhere?"

Herbie was taken aback. "How'd ya' know my fuckin' name? An' how'd ya' know what I was thinkin'?"

"You've hardly got too much going on up there so it's nice and easy to tap in," said Marc.

"Pammy's got even less going on in her head than you do. She's trying to figure out who Herbie is," said Phil.

Herbie could feel the vein in his temple throbbing. "Give us ya' fuckin' money now, or I'll cut ya' ugly faces."

The guys remained unmoved.

"An' how'd ya' know my name? I don't got it written on my face."

"Drop your pants and we'll check for you," said Sumo.

The guys laughed and Kam handed out another round.

Herbie eyed the beer hungrily.

"Give him one," said Tash, "see if he can handle it."

Kam tossed him a can. His fingers went to where the ring-pull should have been but nothing was there. He turned the can over; still nothing. "How do ya' open the fuckin' thing," he asked all agitated.

"You don't," lied Tash. "You bite a couple of holes into the top and drink away."

Herbie tried with all might to break through the titanium magnesium alloy but his loose, rotting teeth just weren't up to it. He should have listened to his mother and brushed twice a day and gone to the dentist regularly when he was a kid, but he hated the sound of the drill - it scared him - so his gums were full of old pretzels and bagels and his teeth flapped in the breeze.

"Fuckin' can, fuckin' stupid can," he yelled. "I can't fuckin'..." In sheer frustration he threw the can into the bushes.

Herbie watched the guys effortlessly unscrew the top of the can and drink the contents as if out of a wide rimmed glass. He had never seen anything like it before. He stood there dumbstruck, which was not a difficult thing.

Meanwhile, Pammy was so busy with the whole Herbie thing she'd missed the rest of the exchange. Being with a guy named Herbie suddenly bothered her. She thought he was cool when his name was Venom X, now she wasn't so sure about him and he did smell. He stunk like old wet socks that had been trapped in a pair of running shoes during a long, cold winter in Maine. Maybe it was time for a wash.

The guys were quite amused by the little game they were playing but Herbie was getting impatient. He started moving around in an irritated fashion, like a druggie who needed a fix. Who the hell was he dealing with here? They knew his name and they had strange beer cans and they looked odd. One of 'em had real busy eyebrows and the others didn't have any, but the guy with the brows had some cool lookin' threads on. He ran his hand over his face and decided to try a different approach.

"OK," he said, in as calm a manner as he could muster, "here's the deal. You give me an' Pammy all your valuables, includin' the drinks, an' we'll let ya' go without touchin' ya', OK."

"We can't do that Herb, old boy. You see, we have no valuables and we're on a buck's night so we definitely can't give up our drinks. That's a strict rule we must follow - once you start drinking it you gotta finish it even if it tastes as bad as an old lady's undies after a day at the bingo hall," Joc informed him. "We only brought enough with us for a short walk to the nearest bar."

"Well here's my rules. You're on my turf, ya' got no permission from me so I can takes what I want, you got it?"

"You're not listening Herbie, we're not gonna give you a thing," said Marc. He turned to the others. "How's about we convince Herb here that we mean it. We got partying to do and this is getting us nowhere."

With the combined force of their telepathic powers the guys invaded Herbie's brain. There was so much vacant space for rent he could have built an apartment complex complete with community pool and fully equipped gymnasium. It was a pity he didn't have any business sense.

Herbie stood there not knowing what was happening to him. He heard a thousand voices and suggestions for auto-anal intrusion and kinky things to do with squirrels.

Herbie's mind went into information overload and abruptly switched off. He'd blown a fuse. Every neuron ached and his senses were addled. The guys stopped transmitting. Their mission was accomplished. Pammy gazed into the distance and dreamed of meeting a man with a name she could relate to, something like Poison Z. Her mind wasn't terribly inventive. She'd sneak away from Herbie later tonight, when he was asleep, and seek out another soul mate. She sighed wistfully. She was glad to have a purpose.

Herbie didn't move a muscle. He couldn't. He had visions of fairies dancing in his head and he suddenly realised he wanted a career as a ballerina. He'd always liked those tutus. He'd sneak away from Pammy later tonight, when she was asleep, and go to Juilliard School of Dance and sign up. He felt good now, but why couldn't he move? How was he ever going to pirouette?

"It's OK Herb, you'll be as good as new in about ten minutes. Be sure to send us tickets to your debut, won't you," Marc said. "I'm sure you'll be a smash." He gave him a wink.

The guys took another beer and walked on down the path to where the big city beckoned them.

Leaving a man without any defences was a dangerous thing in the Park, but the guys didn't know that, not being residents of the planet and all, so Herbie stood helpless and Pammy stood useless as Zero Care and Code Red mugged them. It was a bad end to a trying night. Herbie was definitely giving this business the big flick. Zero and Code made off with Herbie's knife, twenty bucks, two stale sandwiches, a fake Rolex and some shirt pocket lint. It was a good score.

As they headed into the bushes he heard Zero whoop in delight. He'd found a full can of beer. Good, let him suffer, thought Herbie. He hoped they'd kill each other trying to open the fucking thing. He would have laughed if he could have.

The guys were nearing the end of the Park that came out onto 59th Street and Broadway. They were pleased they'd gotten the chance to experience one of the city's pastimes. Doing so made them realise how easy Earthlings were to manipulate. That was a handy piece of information to have for possible later use. All they needed to do now was cross against the lights and eat something round that came in a paper wrapper and they'd be culturally complete.

As they exited the Park the lights were amazing, but the traffic and its fumes were horrendous. On a Saturday night the city was a noisy place and cabs, cars and buses vied for equal space on roads that just weren't big enough to accommodate them. A sea of people swarmed around every available space on the footpath, with some spilling out onto the road. The guys, having seen some awesome sights in their time from all vantage points, were not especially impressed.

In comparison to Jepatsia on Mars this place was a country town. But they couldn't complain because at least they hadn't been banned from here. This fact alone made the city a good place to be.

"Well we've found the people but where are the nightclubs?" Joc asked, looking around as if one would miraculously appear on a street corner just for him.

"A lot of people are heading that way," said Phil pointing south, "let's follow the crowd."

"And move quickly guys, I'm trying to break a record here and at this rate I'll never do it," complained Sumo. Sumo hadn't felt this strong and determined in ages. Alcohol agreed with him. He agreed with alcohol.

They decided to turn their telepathy switches off until they needed them because with this many people around it would be too hard to send or receive anything effectively. Their telepathy worked best in a completely quiet environment or when eye contact could be made and sustained for at least thirty seconds.

Joining the throng of the crowds the guys noticed that no one looked at them. Groups who were together would look at each other but strangers stared straight through or past them and looked down or around but never up. A couple of people looked at Marc's suit a bit strangely but other than that there was hardly any emotion on the faces of these people who seemed to be in a great hurry to get who knew where. Tash tried to engage a guy sitting on the sidewalk in conversation but all he got for his trouble was a demand for loose change and a request to cut the chit-chat.

Having walked several blocks past flashing lights and loud music without managing to break through the mass of bodies to investigate what was happening, the crowd quite suddenly dispersed. People headed off in ten different directions without missing a single beat. Wherever the guys were now was busy but spread out. Then, like a beacon sent from the long forgotten 'Great One' of Sansutopia, a neon sign flashed at the guys. In four different colours it told them that drinks were available, women were available and women full of drinks were available. Now this was what they'd travelled thirty thousand light years for.

Crossing against the lights, as everybody else was doing, the guys practically ran to the door of the club. An oldish man with a voice box ruined by too many whiskies and cigarettes rasped for the guys to go in. A guy called Bruno would check their IDs. Going in through the splitting wooden doors the guys were hit by the stench of stale piss, beer, smoke, farts, burps and Brylcream, and they were only in the foyer.

"Aah, it's just like my bedroom," said Tash, taking a lung full of foul air.

"I can't smell nothin'," said Sumo. "It must be bad in here."

"It is. But so what?" said Marc. "It's an odour a man can grow to love." He breathed deeply to show that his impending marriage wasn't gonna turn him into no sissy boy. He could enjoy a smell you could chew as well as the next man. For some strange reason he felt like beating his chest and declaring his allegiance to all things macho, so he did. And it felt good. Yep, gotta love being a man, he thought. Now it was drink time and all that stood between them and a chronic hangover was Bruno.

Bruno stood like a Russian Tank waiting to crush everything in its path. He had size sixteen boots and legs like tree trunks but perched on top of his body, which was the size of a small aircraft carrier, was a pin head. What was there of his hair was teased out to try and give the illusion of a bigger cranium, but it did nothing except make him look like a sloth with a pompadour. As no one had ever had the guts to tell him, he brushed and sprayed and coiffed himself a bouffant hairdo every night and went to work a confident man.

Not realising that Bruno was there to stop unsavoury types or minors from entering the inner sanctum of the club, the guys tried to stroll past without disturbing him. A thick hand with skin like a rhinoceros clamped around Joc's shoulder. Joc shrank under the touch.

"IDs," Bruno demanded.

Joc looked up at him. "I'm Joc," he said. "and this is Marc, Phil, Davis, Kam…"

"Don't give me no funny shit," growled Bruno. "IDs."

Joc started again, "I'm Joc…"

"… Hey," Bruno interrupted, "it's Saturday, right? An' I hate gettin' mad on a Saturday 'cos the next day is Sunday an' I hate bein' mad on a Sunday 'cos on Sunday I see my mom an' my mom likes to see me smile, yous got it, so don't mess me around with no bullshit, yous got it?"

"It's actually Sunday now because it's past mid…"

"Like I was sayin', I hate bein' mad on Sunday an' now I can feel my neck gettin' tight. When I can feel that I know I'm gonna perspire next an' perspiration makes me feel uncomfortable, like I'm unclean or somethin', yous got it? So, bein' polite like I am, I'm gonna aks you one more time - IDs."

The guys really needed a drink but they couldn't understand what he wanted. On Dectarus, IDs were names, not mug shots that made you look like your Great Aunt Bertha on Crack, complete with a fake date of birth.

Marc tried. "I'm Marc, this is Phil, Tash…"

"OK, I'm thinkin' that I'm bein' real patient 'cos yous don't look like you come from 'round here 'cos you look like maybe you're Canadian an' I dunno how yous do things up there so I'm gonna explain real slow so's as you get it. OK, I don't wanna know your names, yous got it, I wanna see some IDs - a picture with your name next to it an' some numbers that says yous are over twenty-one. OK, yous got it?"

They got it! But they didn't have any such things.

"I'll take care of this guys," Joc said. He turned his telepathy switch on.

Bruno was thinking about being a rich man and wondering if he'd ever find a market for his rat fur cardigans so, for the rest of his life, he'd never have to deal with wankers and stupid drunken wowsers who loved to pick fights or mess with bouncers just for the hell of it. Everybody was a hero when his mates were around.

Inside his head Bruno suddenly heard a voice and it wasn't his because his voice was talking relief from dick heads and this new voice was telling him to let these guys into the club right now, no questions asked, no IDs. Now why would he think that? He was the second best bouncer in the city and to let these guys straight through would be like buying Dunlop instead of Nike. He just couldn't do it.

Joc had confused Bruno. This was good but he'd have to use a bit of hypnosis on him to get him to bend. Joc didn't really like doing it because a famous study, conducted over a ten year period by Professors Grey, Grey and Grey of Plaedes, had shown that after inducing Earthlings into a mesmerised state, on release from the sleep-like trance their behaviour became increasingly paranoid and irrational and they began to imagine things that weren't really there or they'd turn an easily explained occurrence into a mysterious happening.

A lot of them also suffered from false memory syndrome which had them claiming to have been taken to far away planets and being used in experiments by big-eyed, spindly-armed creatures. Other residents of other planets who also took part in the experiment showed no post-study trauma or change in behaviour. No adequate explanation as to why this kind of misconception occurred amongst Earthlings was ever found.

Mixing his thoughts into Bruno's, Joc told him he was feeling sleepy and that his eyelids were getting heavy. Bruno did a big yawn and closed his eyes. His head slumped forward. Joc went straight for his subconscious. There was some freaky shit going on in there but Joc didn't have time to probe too much because he was dying for a drink. Ten minutes is a long time to go without. Although Bruno's fetish for rubber was quite fascinating and a girl named Delores seemed to be very friendly for fifty bucks, Joc was getting sidetracked so he forced himself to get back to the job at hand.

Inputting thoughts was easy. All you had to do was go via the self-preservation mechanism of the mind otherwise you risked the subject using their internal safeguard function to stop you from making suggestions they didn't like. Fortunately Bruno's function was weak because he quite liked to be controlled, but only by women in spiked heel shoes and only when he was wearing a pink chiffon scarf. Kinky, thought Joc.

Anyway, Joc made Bruno believe all was well with the guys and that a few free drinks would be a very friendly gesture. He was nearly going to convince him he loved wearing feather boa's to Sunday lunch and red lipstick was an essential in every man's wardrobe but he didn't have the heart. Bruno was a harmless guy just trying to do his job. Joc was getting soft.

Joc brought Bruno back around. He opened his eyes and felt quite refreshed. Must be the cranberry juice, he thought, that made him feel so bright and alert. He'd changed his diet two days ago, cutting out caffeine and dairy products because he was putting on weight and his reflexes were slowing down. Bruno looked at the guys. They seemed nice enough, the voice liked them and they all had permission from their moms to be there so he figured - what the hell.

"OK," he said, "go through. Tell Jimmy to give yous anythin' you want, on the house."

He looked confused. Did he just say what he thought he said? Then he couldn't remember what he'd said. Then he couldn't remember that he couldn't remember. Joc guessed he'd be back to normal in about ten minutes if the confusion he was going to experience in the meantime didn't addle him too much.

The guys rushed through the doors in case Bruno suddenly changed his mind, or came to his senses.

Chapter 8

It was dark and small inside the club. The stench was overwhelmingly strong now they were in the thick of it. The guys looked around. There didn't seem to be a single woman in the whole place. There was a catwalk type stage in the middle of the floor and the bar ran along the far wall, to the left of it. A guy, who looked similar to Bruno, lifted a comatose drunk off the floor, dumped him in a chair and ordered him another drink. He rifled his pockets, found his wallet and paid Jimmy the barman, throwing in a hefty tip for service with a smile. That's how Jimmy got most of his tips, and drinks too, because they were never drunk by the poor schmuck who'd paid for them.

All up there were about twenty forlorn looking men in the place. Some sat alone nursing drinks and some sat in groups trying to make themselves heard over the awful music that crackled out of old speakers. The guys couldn't believe the trouble they'd had to go through to get into this dive.

"If this is the best club this city's got to offer, we're in big trouble," Tash said, looking around.

They made their way to the bar and ordered the strongest drink Jimmy had. He gave them a Jack Daniels each and asked for forty bucks. Joc let him know that drinks were free because Bruno said so. Jimmy shrugged and wiped the bar. Let the boss deal with it when he got back, he thought.

Jimmy hated getting involved in the 'drinks are on the house' kind of scenes. He'd had his nose broken once and half his ear ripped off and he wasn't keen to go through that again because he hated hospitals. He'd gone in to be fixed up and they took half his blood and stuck fingers and instruments up every hole testing for who knew what. He'd spent four hours waiting in casualty and then spent seven hours being prodded and poked. They found places he never knew he had. The only good thing to come out of the visit was the enema. He'd been constipated for near on two weeks, that was partly why he was so cranky and had ended up in a brawl, and to suddenly be eight pounds lighter was an incredible relief. Nowadays he drank prune juice and ate bran. It kept him calmer and happier.

Before they'd finished their first drink, they ordered another round. "So Jimmy," Joc asked, "where are the women?"

"There's another show in about ten minutes," he answered. Jimmy wandered off and served a paying customer.

The guys sat down at a table and waited for the women to show. As they complained about the drinks being weak, Kam remembered he'd brought a couple of bottles of Black Howack with him. Now that was a smooth drop. He pulled a bottle out of the knapsack and their eyes lit up, relieved they had some good stuff. Glasses were filled and contentment flowed down their throats.

The booze had a calming effect on Sumo for about twenty seconds and then he started getting impatient. He wanted naked women and he didn't wanna have to wait. He hadn't seen naked flesh since his buck's night. His wife's flesh didn't count. "We shoulda stayed home and gone to the Brainsmasher. They got women 'round the clock."

"Yeah, but we don't hafta pay for the women here," Joc said. "Have another drink."

Sumo did. And he was OK for another twenty seconds. He thrust his hand out for more and Kam poured another double serve of Howack, which Sumo promptly shot down his throat.

Joc picked up a handful of stale nuts from the bowl that was glued to the middle of the table and threw them at Kam. He pointed at his empty glass. Kam began doing the rounds and just as Joc was shouting for him to fill his glass to the top, a high-pitched squeal preceded the merciful death of the music. Joc's voice bounced around the room.

This prompted the Bruno look alike to direct his gaze at their table. If there was one thing he couldn't stand it was seein' more than four young guys together at any one time. It usually meant trouble. Well if they wanted trouble, they'd come to the right place because he didn't take no shit from no one. Sure, people had tried it on him before but he was no pushover. He didn't spend three hours a day at the gym for nothin'.

Normally he liked the opportunity to flex his muscles, when he could, but tonight he had a headache. His marriage was going out the window and his wife was taking him to court to get the apartment. It was his girlfriend's fault. If she hadn't found out he was married then gotten chummy with his wife, none of this would've happened. Women! You couldn't trust 'em.

He strolled over to the guys and stood next to Joc. He liked to think he looked foreboding.

"How you doing Benny?" Joc enquired, with his biggest smile.

"How'd ya' know my name? I never tol' ya' my name," he said all tough like. Friendly greeting or not, this was a strip joint. No plush carpets and clean toilets here. No room for niceties.

"Bruno told us," lied Phil.

"Oh." He was taken aback. "Anyways, I'm just checkin' that yous are gonna behave yourselfs so's I don't gotta get rough. OK?"

"OK. Not a problem." Davis's mouth had gone dry. "We'll just sit here quietly and wait for the women."

"Good. I'm gonna be over there watchin' ya's, so keep ya' noses clean." Benny walked back to where he'd come from.

"Whoa," said Joc, "way too many 'roids in him."

They laughed - discreetly - and quaffed Howack openly.

Jimmy was trying to fix the music. Every now and then there would be a boom or bam at ear splitting level and then silence. When the music first died, conversations around them fell to a whisper but now that it had been off for five minutes voices started rising again and it became increasingly obvious that drunken ramblings didn't exactly contain Nobel Prize winning ideas.

At the next table two guys were discussing sitcoms. The discussion must have become heated because the one guy was practically shouting at the other. Either that or he'd had the very combination of drinks that made it happen naturally.

"It don't matter which show ya' mention, it's always the same," drunk number one yelled. He poked the air with his finger and attempted to explain the incalculable number of similarities but his brain couldn't produce any words to go with the action. Getting nowhere, he changed his thought track to words his brain could produce and called to Jimmy for two more beers then turned his attention back to his favourite topic.

"Where was I? Oh yeah, see I'm right. Them TV people got one script an' different people say the same stuff an' do the same stuff. They just change the names, that's all."

Jimmy brought them a couple of Bud's. "How's your missus, Tony?" he asked drunk number one. "You spend more time here than at home."

"She's OK. Anyway, the girls here are better lookin' an' they don't make me take out the garbage."

"That's 'cos here, you are the garbage," Jimmy laughed. He felt he was entitled to insult the patrons because ... well, just because. Benny wandered over to make sure all was well. It was, so he crawled back to his safety zone.

Tony now felt ready to elaborate on each and every similarity but he didn't know where to begin so he drank his beer to give him time to think. His mate Sam was happy not to have to listen to the same old bullshit he put up with every time they got together. Now that Tony had cable the problem was getting worse because repeats of old shows that should have been long forgotten popped up again for Tony to study in great depth. Sam lamented the tragedy of a life spent in front of the tube. Sam would have gone to another bar but he hated drinking alone. Tony's company was better than none in this big, lonely city.

Opening the second bottle of Howack, Kam poured a generous drop for each of them.

"I'm gonna get some more of that Jack Daniels." Harri approached Jimmy and got him to hand over a full bottle.

The two drinks were mixed and the combination became a slimy green colour. "It looks like the colour of a Trolgians teeth," said Tash.

"You'd know," said Harri. "You kissed one."

"Don't remind me." Tash suddenly felt a bit sick as he remembered the kiss. It was the first time anyone had shown an interest in him and who was he to say no. If he'd known the green was actually an algae used as a breeding ground for tiny Hesper Wasps he would have thought twice. Closing his eyes, so as not to have to look at the colour, he took a mouthful. It tasted better than it looked. Not much better but taste wasn't an issue, potency was. And it packed a punch.

Just as Tony started discussing the merits of cop shows, the music came back on. Tony's voice was drowned out, which was a relief for everyone within earshot. A yellow spotlight lit up an area of the stage and a voice came through the speakers introducing the very beautiful and talented Sugar Anne all the way from Indiana, and urging the crowd - all twenty of them - to make her welcome. The voice stopped. The music stopped. The spotlight wavered unsteadily as it focused on the back of the stage.

With a terrific crashing sound, 'I Can't Wait', by Stevie Nicks, blasted out of the crackly speakers and reverberated off the walls. Staring at the stage the guys waited for Sugar Anne. She was certainly taking her sweet time. Joc banged his fists on the table and yelled "Sugar, Sugar, Sugar." The others joined him, as did Tony, Sam and three or four others who were still sober enough to care about her appearance.

Benny didn't like the way those young guys were stirring up emotions amongst the men. He moved a bit closer to their table to keep a keener eye on them. At the first sign of trouble he'd pounce like a cat. He breathed deeply, anticipating trouble; tasting it even. He could never work in one of those trendy, up market nightclub-cum-caffé-latté-cum-spaghetti-cum-owned-by-famous-people places. There was never any trouble in those clean, preppy establishments. Nope, he liked it here. He was born to be here. Besides, he liked the naked women.

Sugar Anne finally made her entrance. She'd missed her cue because she'd forgotten to put on her hat and the hat was half her act. Her memory wasn't the best lately. Too many late nights and early mornings. Coming into her first song a full minute late she had to fling off her jacket without any of the usual teasing. Her footwork was out of sync but she knew she'd be the only one to notice. Theses guys didn't come to check out her Arthur Murray moves.

She was of medium build with strong, muscly legs and big forearms. Her stilettos looked like they belonged on a woman half her size. Still, she managed to dance in them. A pair of bike boots would have suited her better and then maybe her calves wouldn't have constantly ached or cramped up. A frozen smile was fixed on her face. Another crummy crowd, she thought. Tipping would be lousy.

Prancing up and down the catwalk she twisted and turned, bent forwards, backwards, sideways, all ways. The guys were beside themselves. Her hat came off to reveal an over-sprayed, stiff hairdo. She flicked her head and her hair bounced slightly. Turning her back on her audience she relaxed the smile and exercised her jaw to get some feeling back into it.

000 80 000

Turning back, smile intact again, she used her hat like an Olympic gymnast uses a ball. She flung it up high, did the splits, caught it, rolled it across her arms, threw it on the floor and tumbled towards it picking it up between her thighs. She arched her back, supported herself on one arm, gyrated her hips, pushed the hat underneath her skirt and rubbed it against her G-string. Laying back flat on the floor she did some fancy things with her upright legs and writhed around a bit until the song changed.

To the strains of Pat Benatar's version of 'I Need A Lover', Sugar stood up and guided the hat back up her torso. Holding it against her breasts she reached behind with her other hand, unsnapped her bra and flung it towards the back of the catwalk. Dozens of eyes stared hungrily as she brought her head forward, put the brim of the hat in her mouth, flicked it into the air, spun around, so as not to show too much too soon, and expertly caught the hat on her head. She pranced away.

The guys cheered and screamed. They were getting louder than the music and the heat in the place felt like it had gone up twenty degrees Celsius, which in actual fact it had. Jimmy had turned up the thermostat to get the patrons to buy more drinks. It was designed to make it look as if Sugar Anne was making them sweat and it worked every time.

Slowly, Sugar moved backwards down the catwalk towards her lascivious audience, arms outstretched either side of her. Stopping near the end she dropped her arms, covered her breasts with her hands, turned around to face them and stood perfectly still. Surveying the audience for someone to titillate up close she didn't look further than Kam. In the dark of the club he appeared to be nice looking although it was not uncommon for veritable freaks to come across as this year's model in this kind of lighting. Still, choices were limited. Three hours earlier the place had been packed, now all she could see was a bunch of stragglers who were too drunk to get out of their chairs.

After waiting for, and getting, the obligatory chant of the primal kind urging her to move her hands and get the rest of her gear off, Sugar made her way towards Kam. The guys knew she was coming to them and they nearly exploded with the excitement. The J. D. and Howack had caused quite a chemical reaction in their brains. They were drunk. Officially and unequivocally drunk. No longer were they half way there or feeling tipsy merely teetering on the edge of stuporous inertia, they were pissed out of their heads. And it felt good, damn good.

Sugar sashayed her way between the tables, teasing the regulars as she went. She realised that going over to a table full of young guys was a risk because they tended to want to grab and maul any exposed flesh, but she was a bit sick of doing her act to old men who had watery eyes and bad beer breath.

Doing a complete circle of their table she was glad she'd made Kam her choice because he was quiet too. The other seven were all yelling at the same time and pointing at the guy with the weird eyebrows. Even in this light he looked like a loony. Joc stood up to try and get her attention to tell her to give Marc some extra special treatment but he fell over. By the time he'd gotten up she was running her hands over Kam's face. Lucky bastard.

Sugar had nice, firm, round breasts which were practically in Kam's face, with decorative silver dangly bits in the centre of them. Marc thought perhaps she'd had those put on when she'd had the silicon put in. Silicon was popular on Dectarus too. Actually, it was popular a lot of places. Whoever the salesperson for it was, was doing a fine job of spreading it around. He bet their end of year bonus was quite substantial.

Taking Kam by the hand, Sugar pulled him out of his chair and led him back to the stage. The guys went wild. Kam looked confused. It wasn't his buck's night so why was he going instead of Marc? Sitting him down on the edge of the stage, Sugar sat behind him, wrapped her legs around his waist and ran her hands up and down his torso, being careful to avoid his crotch but making it look as if she was stroking that area too. She couldn't believe how uncontrollable this sent his mates. They were probably all virgins.

With a deft movement she clamped her thighs hard around his lower rib cage and in a wrestling manoeuvre the WWE would have been proud of, she dragged Kam backwards and flipped him over onto his front. She was a strong girl. The muscles in her thighs were like iron. Kam was in love. Holding him down with her arms she pulled her leg out from underneath him and lay on top of his body. They were facing the audience.

Grabbing his arms she pinned them behind his back, as if he were being arrested for disorderly behaviour, and held his wrists with one hand. Kam didn't even attempt to struggle. With the other hand she grabbed his hair and lifted his head up so he could see his mates cheering and clapping. Man those guys were loud. She sat up on his lower back and bucked up and down as if she were riding a horse. Kam couldn't ever remember having such a good time. He wondered if she was single and if so, if she'd consider marrying him.

Song number two was coming to an end so Sugar had to move things along a bit. Standing up she placed one foot on Kam's back, moved her body around so she was facing away from her audience, undid the one snap fastener that held her skirt together and danced the satin material across her buttocks. From the roar that went up you would have thought she was doing a concert in Madison Square Garden for the entire city of New York. As the third and final song began, which was Blondie's 'In The Flesh', she slowed down her tempo.

Taking her skirt in one hand and swirling it around above her head she ditched it to the back of the stage to keep her bra company. There was that roar again. She had a great arse and she knew it. Bending forward, much to the appreciation of the guys, she rolled Kam over so he was on his back and staring straight up between her legs. Her G-string matches her eyes, Kam thought romantically. Falling down over his body Sugar did six slow push-ups.

Joc was finding it hard to control himself but he knew Benny was keeping a close eye on him just waiting for him to do something that would warrant a fight, so he restrained himself.

Sugar leant on her arms and dragged the lower half of her body past Kam's face. She almost doubled herself up and then raised her body until she was standing erect. Offering her hand to Kam she pulled him up off the floor, put her arm around his shoulder and pulled him into a half hug, made him bow and told him to go and sit back down. As Kam started to leave the stage she slapped his bum. He nearly tripped and fell as he stood down. His mind was in a love haze. One of her hairs was sticking to his top lip. He pulled it away and carefully placed it in his pocket. He planned to frame it when he got home.

Strutting back up the catwalk, Sugar finished her act with a few gyrations and by pretending she was going to rip her G-string off. A couple of gymnastic moves later, she was done. Then before Kam had a chance to really enjoy her last moments, she was gone, swallowed up by the big curtain. He felt lost and alone. He had another drink to help him forget.

The crappy music started up again and the same voice as before announced that in five minutes there would be another dancer for their entertainment; to have another drink, settle down and get ready to be hot and bothered all over again.

"This is too tetra," shouted Joc. "They got another one coming out."

In his relatively short life, Joc had been to at least a hundred planets and seen scientific phenomenon that by Earth's standards just wasn't possible. He'd seen dozens of different life forms, partaken of rare and exotic food and drink, travelled faster than the speed of light, he possessed the brain of a mega-mega genius - when he bothered to exercise it, always kept up with the latest fashions and was popular with everybody he met because he was smooth and likeable and yet, everything paled in comparison to a show of flesh and a hint of sex from an almost naked woman. He turned into a drooling juvenile with the I.Q. of a gnat and the decorum of a wild boar that had just been shot in the rump by a grossly inadequate first time hunter using a .45 calibre handgun.

Unfortunately no study had been conducted into why this type of thing was common amongst most males of most life forms. Funding was never made available because no one really wanted to explain it. The team from the department of 'Study into Irrational, Childish and Kinky Behaviour' feared the answer might somehow alter or ruin the delicate balance of nature. Some things were better left uninvestigated and to try and bring it back to a science was deemed an unnecessary waste of time and resources. The money saved from canning the project went, instead, to the 'Manipulating Statistics so Your Bell Curve is Evenly Distributed' department.

Statisticians were pleased about this because if there was one thing they couldn't tolerate it was too many people falling outside of the norm. Their next study was to determine exactly what the norm was and how they could fit everybody into the wide bit of the bell. It was an exciting time for all concerned.

Kam poured the last of the J. D. and Black Howack into his glass and drank it down in one gulp. Before, his mind had been like a foggy afternoon in the north of Scotland, now it was like a rainy winter's day in Paris with nowhere to go and no money to buy fresh bread and cheese. He didn't care. All he cared about was Sugar's thighs and her incredible athletic ability. Women on Dectarus never did things like she did. He wondered what would happen if he decided to stay here in New York. Would anybody notice an illegal alien? All he knew for sure was that he needed another drink.

"Joc, go and get another bottle of something," Marc managed to slur.

"D'ya want the same stuff or something different?"

"We don't care," said Tash, "anything'll do."

Joc made a bee-line for the bar. Jimmy was talking to Benny and a short, fat guy with greasy, slicked back hair and more wrinkles than an unironed shirt that had been lost in a hotel laundry hamper for a year.

Jimmy was pointing at Joc and past him to the guys. Joc didn't like the look of this. Act casual, he thought.

He stood at the bar waiting for Jimmy to finish his conversation and tried to use his telepathy to hone in on what was being discussed. They weren't quite close enough to get a clear reception and the noise coming from the speakers didn't help. All he could get was an annoying yeah, yeah, from Benny.

The walking crows feet started nodding his head. He patted Jimmy on the arm and approached Joc. Now Joc could pick up what he was going to say and it wasn't gonna be good.

"Jimmy tells me you an' your boys been drinkin' free booze. Is that right?"

"Bernardo, here's the thing …"

"… How'd ya' know my name? I never told ya' my name."

Why did that sound familiar? "Benny told me. He told me what a great Pop you are to him and Bruno, giving them jobs in the business. You're a good and decent man."

"He said that? Geez, your kids don't tell ya' to your face these things. They gotta tell 'em to strangers. Didn't I bring 'em up right?"

Bernardo looked contemplative for a moment. He was thinking about his wife Berniece and how the boys always openly showed their affection for her. She'd always said that patience brought its own rewards. Maybe he oughta stop yellin' at 'em so much but sometimes they were so stupid he couldn't help himself.

"Anyways, like I was sayin' - Jimmy says that you says Bruno says it's OK to have drinks for nothin'. Is that right?"

"Kinda, yeah. You see, we don't come from here and we got no money to pay for drinks, so we hadda say they were free so we could keep up our level of drunkenness."

"Mmm. I can see you're bein' honest but I don't like bein' ripped off so I'm gonna hafta kick ya' outta here an' I'm gonna hafta hurt ya' while me an' my boys are doin' it, OK? I'm tellin' ya' so's ya' don't try an' sue me for grievous bodily harm or loss of enjoyment or somethin' stupid like that, OK? I'll give ya' a minute to tell your friends an' then we'll be on ya'. OK?"

Joc didn't want to leave yet and definitely not before the next stripper came out. He'd have to use hypno. Joc worked hard to focus his drunken, muddled thoughts. He concentrated on getting Bernardo to agree to letting them stay and give them as many free drinks as they wanted. Unwittingly, Joc also probed the old lecher's mind. It seemed Bernardo had the hots for one of his girls, someone called Brandy Snap, but she had told him to lose weight and stop eating garlic and then she might not find him so repulsive. He hoped the diamond he'd bought her would help make him more attractive. Joc seriously doubted that.

Joc was about twenty seconds into the convincing process, and Bernardo was responding very nicely, when those broken down old speakers made a shrill noise loud enough to wake the dead. Joc's thoughts were abruptly cut off by the booming music that followed the squeal. A loud voice introducing Candy Apple filled Bernardo's head. Now it was going to be impossible for Joc to get in and finish the suggestions. Being interrupted was not good.

Bernardo blinked and looked confused. He felt that time had stopped for a moment. He remembered that he was thinking that Joc and his pals were OK and they should have the run of the bar but why he would even think anything like that was beyond him. Even his sons paid for their own drinks. Bernardo eyed Joc suspiciously. Suddenly he didn't care if he had been honest and he didn't like the fact the guy had no eyebrows. It wasn't natural. It was time to haul their sorry asses outta there.

Chapter 9

Candy Apple smiled and cavorted her way around the stage. Marc drooled. Kam was uninterested. Nothing could compare to Sugar Anne. From out of nowhere, Joc crash landed on top of their table.

"Where's the drinks?" Phil asked.

"Forget the drinks, we gotta get outta here before Bernardo and his boys kill us. Move it."

"But what about Candy? Just look at those norks would you," Sumo said.

Before Joc had a chance to slide off the table Benny pounced on him, grabbed his shirt collar and pulled him up hard.

"Guys," rasped Joc, "now would be a good time to help me."

The guys tutted. What a bloody inappropriate moment to start a brawl.

Phil stood up and grabbed hold of Benny's arm. It was clear the guy was not made of flesh and blood because his arm felt like a pile of house bricks. To cop a forearm in the jaw would not be a pleasant experience. Phil told the others to grab on somewhere.

Benny shook Joc like a rag doll while the guys tried to shake Benny, but he stood firm. Not even a Mack truck could have knocked him down.

Benny dragged Joc towards the door while the others stumbled along with them, unable to stop the marauding machine of a man. Bernardo watched and waited to see if Benny would need any help but he was carrying all the guys along with no effort at all.

Candy continued on, seemingly oblivious to the trouble. When you worked in strip joints long enough you saw all sorts of stuff so nothing fazed you in the end. But with the guys on their way out there was hardly anyone worth performing for. She let her smile slip and felt the tension drain from her cheeks. That was much better.

"Guys, I'm being strangled here." Joc's face was going red and he wasn't breathing as much as he should have been.

"We're doing the best we can," said Tash, "but this guy's made of stone."

In a brave move, or rather a 'I'm drunk so I'm tough now' move, Davis grabbed hold of Benny's hair. Benny screamed and let Joc go. Joc fell onto the floor and Benny accidentally trod on him with his Yeti feet as he staggered around clutching the top of his head. Really, Davis had hardly touched him but Benny was practically sobbing. Davis had a hand full of hair and Benny had a bald patch on his crown. He couldn't understand how it had come away so easily as he hadn't even tugged. This was not good.

"My plugs! Pop," Benny yelled at the top of his voice, "Pop, they pulled my plugs out."

Bernardo ran over. "Now how's he gonna save his marriage when he's got no hair? Yous idiots are gonna pay. Benny, it's OK," he soothed, "we'll get ya' some more. They weren't takin' too good anyways. We'll sue the place ya' bin goin' to and we'll send ya' somewhere better. Finish takin' out the trash and then we'll fix ya' up, OK."

"OK Pop." Benny looked like a four year old who'd just grazed his knee and was promised a lolly if he smiled.

Joc's kidney had practically been squashed flat by Benny's less than delicate stomp. Tash and Harri helped him up while Sumo stood mesmerised and watched Candy go through her routine. No doubt about it, he could definitely learn to appreciate a girl like that. He thought of Sotty and shivered.

Benny decided to get rough. He was through being gentle and playful. Eight wimps should have been easy to handle; a piece of cake, but he'd let his guard down. "Can I hurt 'em Pop?" he asked.

"Sure, why not. Anyways, I already warned 'em they'd get hurt so it's OK."

"Thanks Pop." Benny smiled again.

Davis was the first to feel the hands of death touch him. Helplessly he tried offering Benny his hair back but seeing his three thousand dollar strands in the hands of a delinquent only enraged him further. Benny put a finger up Davis's nose and yanked his nostril as far left as it would go. Davis yelled and went skittering sideways through the swing doors into the entrance foyer. He landed at Bruno's feet.

Sumo was still watching Candy shake her hot body into a sweat so when Benny grabbed him he was defenceless and unprepared. With the strength of ten men Benny picked Sumo up, lifted him over his head and threw him out to join Davis.

Kam was backing away towards the doors so Benny gave him a powerful shove to show he was in charge of chucking them out and that none of them were going to escape unharmed. Kam landed on top of Sumo. Bruno looked at the guys and started to get curious as to why they were coming through the doors and falling on top of each other. Maybe he'd go and have a look at what was goin' down.

Bruno nearly made it inside the club but Tash and Harri came flying by and smashed into him on their way out. The three of them fell heavily and Harri's finger somehow found its way into Bruno's ear.

There was no way Phil, Joc and Marc were going to get past the raging Benny. He was on a roll and he had set his sights on eight targets and eight targets were what he was going to eliminate.

He stood in front of the guys in a half crouched position, like a cougar waiting to pounce. He wiggled his hands in a come and get me gesture. "OK, who's next?"

The guys all pointed to each other.

"You choose, Pop."

"Take the guy with the bushy brows an' the weird suit. He don't look like he's right to me."

Marc tried to side step around Benny but the guy was as wide as Trump Towers. No amount of dodging or weaving allowed Marc to get past him. Benny's vice-like grip burned into Marc's upper arm. Lifting him two feet off the ground he swung him around as if he were preparing to toss a discus. Marc was relieved when he went crashing through the doors and got elbowed in the ribs by Harri. He was even more relieved when he fell over and hit the ground because, at the moment, laying down beat trying to stand up. It was a pity the protection suit didn't protect against physical abuse.

Phil and Joc decided to charge Benny at the same time. They hoped they could get enough oomph to knock him down. As it turned out it was a bad move. Grabbing each of them under an armpit and pressing extra hard because of their foolish attempt at trying to hurt him, Benny decided to hold them there for a slow count of ten or until their eyes watered, whichever came first.

Their eyes were watering by number two but Benny was pumped so he held them for the full ten. Phil had gone numb and Joc was seeing little coloured spots. Tossing them slightly into the air Benny hooked his arms around their waists and held them horizontally. Walking to the doors Benny, not too gently, used their heads to push them open. He strolled passed the others, who were rubbing one sore spot or another, and tossed Joc and Phil out onto the sidewalk.

He dusted his hands and his jacket and looked back at the others.

The guys quickly joined Joc and Phil before Benny hurt them further. Bernardo and Benny looked satisfied.

Bruno looked at his brother with shining admiration. Not only was he the smart one, he was the tough one too. He knew how to deal with all types, and deal with them he did. That's why his Pop had him working inside the club. Bruno knew in his heart that some day he'd be workin' for Benny, even if his cardigans made him rich in the meantime, and he'd be the one doin' the clean up jobs. He looked forward to that day with anticipation.

Out on the street the guys picked Joc and Phil up. None of them felt very well. Their heads were spinning and each of them had a throbbing pain somewhere, but nothing was broken. The extra adrenaline they'd just produced had sobered them up slightly. That was the worst thing. Sumo wondered if Candy was naked yet while Kam pined for Sugar Anne. All he needed was a quick shot of Bonala Amber and he was guaranteed to forget all about her. B. Amber erased more memories than an enquiry into the whereabouts of a bankrupt businessman's former fortune but it was selective when mixed with Binzi Glow because then it only targeted painful love memories.

The guys looked around.

"Well, that was fun. Where we gonna go now?" asked Harri.

"Somewhere where there's no viral, barometric guy who might wanna kill us for getting a few free drinks," said Joc.

"Let's start walking and see where we end up," Tash suggested.

The guys limped their way across the road to get away from Bernardo's club. Kam dragged his heels. Sumo just wanted to see more naked women. The night was wearing on and they'd hardly gotten Marc into any trouble and he was still in one piece. They'd have to do something about that pretty soon.

Chapter 10

The streets were alive with activity. Men stood in doorways of shops and clubs calling for passers-by to go in. The guys decided they'd go a bit further down the road yet to get as far away from Bernardo's as possible. Several people stood in front of an electrical goods store watching a news broadcast. The guys stopped to see what was of such interest.

Davis started to sweat. There in living colour was the obscene shape the guys had made in the wheat field at Yorkshire. "We've been found out," he said.

"Relax," said Joc. "We're miles away from that place. They'll never pin it on us. We are miles away, aren't we Phil?"

"Yeah, at least several thousand."

Davis wasn't convinced.

The shot went from the field to a farmer and his cow. The farmer was saying something but the volume on the TV was turned down so they couldn't hear him. From the farmer the scene changed to a woman with a nervous disposition and hair a rat could nest in. She said something too, but the words were lost.

Following her was an effeminate guy wearing an outrageously loud shirt who was gesticulating wildly with his hands in an annoying way. He pointed upwards and made an elongated shape. He clutched his head and shook it as if he was trying to dislodge something from his ears. He looked panicky and pale. He only looked pale because his agent had told him to wear white pancake make-up for added effect.

A quick shot of the reporter showed a blonde woman, who was wearing too much lipstick and eye shadow, nodding her head sympathetically as if she understood perfectly what Mr Obnoxious Clothing was on about.

The news studio cut him off mid-sentence and returned to the anchors. Smiling broadly, Mr. and Mrs. Lift, Tuck, Silicone and Bleach tried to effect a look of concern; the usual look that was reserved for stories about funerals and small animals lost down wells. They cut to a commercial.

"I wonder what that was all about?" Joc said. He would have used his telepathy to get what they were saying but there was no point. Every time in the past he'd tried to read the thoughts of someone on the box all he'd gotten was a buzzing and crackling noise that sounded like a transistor calling for help because it was being fried to death by slow and painful means.

"Crop circles, man, made by aliens," said a scruffy looking guy standing next to Kam. "Probably checkin' out the planet, gettin' ready to invade us an' eat our brains an' stuff," he spluttered nervously. A small trickle of saliva ran down his chin.

Yeah right. Where'd he get his information?

"We're gonna get arrested." Davis whispered furiously. "They'll know it was us. We're the only aliens around here." He would have run if his legs hadn't turned to jelly.

"Davis, did that Redfin bite your balls off?" Tash asked.

"No."

"Well it might as well have, 'cos you don't use them. Take a good look around. The cops could finger most of this lot as being aliens."

Davis looked around and had to agree. A bunch of freaks walked the streets of the city. The guys looked more human than most of the humans. And they had better hair. His nerves settled down. He was a sure-fire candidate for an ulcer and he suffered from dyspepsia as it was.

"OK, we got nothing to worry about," said Harri.

"Yeah, except getting another drink," said Marc.

"Naked women. I gotta see naked women," Sumo added desperately.

"D'ya know any good nightclubs where we can get women and drinks?" Joc asked the scruffy guy.

"Not me man, I never go anywhere. I just like hangin' 'round here an' watchin' the news an' stuff." He turned his attention back to the TV.

"Let's leave this guy to his full and exciting life then," Joc said. "Come on, we'll just keep walking."

They carried on down the street, weaving and bumping into each other as they went. Having relaxed somewhat, the alcohol in their bodies had come out of hiding and gone back to work.

The guys were unsteady on their feet but they thought they were OK. They were too drunk to know they were drunk and they still fully intended to go and get drunk, even though they were that now but didn't know it. It was unfortunate the way a drunk person's mind worked, believing that the brain was a hundred percent comprehensible and the tongue and body were fully functional when in actual fact they were far from it. It was a tricky situation but, because the drunk person in question didn't know it was tricky, they remained blissfully unaware of the anomaly.

Even more fortunate was that the average drunk person didn't know about the word anomaly, or what it meant, and because they didn't know such a word existed they couldn't be affected or confused by an incongruity that didn't exist. It was this simple logic that kept all drinkers happy whilst allowing them to get drunker and drunker without the bother of being concerned about how they looked, sounded, or smelt.

The night air in the city was cool and, because the buildings were so tall, the pollution from the excessive traffic had nowhere to go; even the wind didn't have the strength to pick it up and carry it away. And Tash's own personally produced wind certainly wasn't helping the pollution problem. Every time he drank anything that contained malt or gremphor his digestive system went into turmoil and produced noxious emissions and tonight he'd drunk enough to keep him the life of the party for a fortnight. It was little wonder he wasn't married and had not so much as a prospect in sight.

Whilst searching for their next port of call Sumo suddenly decided they were meandering and not making a good enough effort to get anywhere.

"We gotta get to a bar right now," he said aggressively.

Yes sir.

"You weaklings aren't gonna stop me getting that title."

No sir.

"I gotta seize the day so move your nancy arses."

Fuck you, sir.

"Fine." said Phil, "How about we take fifty giant steps and go into the place we end up nearest. Does that suit you?"

Sumo grunted.

Looking like a bunch of escaped loonies from the asylum for Monty Python fans, the guys stepped awkwardly down the road. Taking too big a step right onto a pile of teflon coated dog poo, Harri's right foot slid along the path at about forty clicks an hour getting him stuck between a nut crush and a nut crunch.

The crotch of his jeans pressed up tight against his dangly bits, crunching them painfully, whilst the pavement threatened to crush them if he slipped down any lower. He was stuck in a muscle pulling, jeans splitting position and the doggy doo filled up the gaps in the sole of his shoe. Although he couldn't appreciate their value at this moment in time, it was actually the tightness of his jeans that kept his nuts hovering above certain death because his legs couldn't spread any further apart.

The guys stood perfectly still, as if in suspended animation, and stared stupidly at Harri and then, as if on cue, they all started laughing at the same time. He waved his arms from side to side in a desperate attempt to keep himself balanced. That only made the guys laugh harder.

A woman in a black and white zebra print skirt threw Harri a quarter as she passed by. She thought he was a busker. Phil picked it up and put it in his pocket. He'd take it home for his old man. It might be worth something.

A man wearing an old brown blanket called Harri a lousy mime and told him to get a real job instead of sponging off the people of New York. He gave him a shove as he stormed on down the street shouting out for all to hear about freeloaders and worthless, useless people turning the city into a cesspit of corruption and crime. Insanity ran in his family, as did hairy ears, ingrown toenails and bad attitudes.

Harri toppled over onto his side and landed heavily on his left shoulder, where a stone buried itself painfully. His legs were frozen in the splits position and refused to relax. A lump of dog shit fell from the side of his shoe.

It was official now - everything hurt. Absolutely and completely. He thought he was sore before but it was nothing compared to what his body was going through now. The only other time in his life when his whole body had hurt like this was when he was six and he'd wet his pants. He'd let his brother put him in the washing machine on the rinse and spin cycle. He didn't make that mistake twice.

Observing the city from his new vantage point, Harri marvelled at how big the buildings were and how dirty the sidewalk was. Quickly getting bored with that, he re-focused on more pressing matters and forced his brain to move his legs into a closed position. Slowly they came together and the muscles relaxed. The tension left his back and he was feeling better.

All he had to do now was get upright and things would be hunky dory.

Joc was the first one to calm down enough to speak. "Are you gonna lie there all night, or what?" he asked. "Move your arse."

"You're lucky I'm alive, never mind anything else. You idiots are about as useful as a devout virgin at a brothel."

Moving carefully, so as to keep the pain to a minimum, Harri rolled onto his elbows and knees and raised himself up slowly.

"Thanks for the helping hand guys. If I'd died you probably would've left me here to get eaten by something feral."

"Stop being so bloody melodramatic," said Sumo. "You slipped on a pile of crap. Big deal. Let's go get a drink, and watch where you walk this time." Since Sumo decided he was going to be the one to break the drinking record he'd become totally focused on his chosen mission and no matter what, he intended to complete it.

"My shoe is full of shit and it stinks. I gotta wipe it off."

"Yeah. You're not getting back on the cruiser until it's gone. Either that or you leave the shoe here," said Phil.

"No way. I got these on Tragda - on sale. I had to beat off an old Leptor for these. I thought she was gonna kill me but I got a good hip and shoulder in and she backed off. Plus they're made from Hum Hum skin and you know that's not easy to come by."

"Part one in the saga of the new shoes continues after this short break," Marc said sarcastically. "Just knock it against something and be quick about it."

Harri looked around for something suitable to use. "That signpost will do." Walking over to the post he kicked it sideways, miscalculated badly and bashed his ankle. He hopped around swearing and cursing.

"Take the shoe off first, you dipshit." Marc rolled his eyes.

"Is this gonna take all night 'cos if it is I'll meet you back here later. I'm not gonna waste good drinking time watching him slowly disable himself," said Sumo, irritably. It had been too long between drinks now and he was not feeling pleased.

"Gimme that shoe," Tash said, yanking it from Harri's foot, "I'll do it. The quicker we get moving, the better."

Tash bashed the shoe against the post. Small amounts of shit came away but a lot of it was firmly embedded in the tread.

"I'd hate to see the size of the animal that dropped that pile," said Davis.

Tash covered his nose with his hand. "It stinks. I wonder what it eats?"

"Same as you, probably," said Kam. "You don't smell any better."

"Ain't that the truth," agreed Marc. "You gotta look at changing your diet. Then you might actually score."

Tash ignored them and bashed away. Harri's shoe was becoming misshapen and the sole was coming away from the side but the shit was falling out in bigger chunks and that was the objective here. The signpost was rattling noisily with each hit. It hadn't started out that noisy but each blow made it a little less stable and a bit more fragile.

Even though the streets were busy, traffic was deafening and people were talking loudly, the one sound that stood out was the bash, bash, bash of the post. It was kind of like being at a boisterous party and yelling to the person you came with that the host always smelt like beer farts just at the very moment everybody stopped talking and the music halted abruptly, whereby you would suddenly become the focus of unwanted attention. Well, the guys were now in just such a situation as hundreds of pairs of eyes turned to see what was going on.

As vandalising a post was hardly newsworthy, most people looked away and carried on with what they were doing. A few stopped to watch the spectacle and fewer still ventured closer to see, first hand, the wilful destruction of public property.

As the sign was indicating a tow away zone the spectators assumed the guys were pissed off out-of-towners who had come back from night-clubbing to find their car had gone and so were trying to rip the post out of the ground. Rebellion always made for exciting viewing and was best watched live.

Two of the interested observers were police officers who walked the streets of the city waiting for any sign of criminal activity. It had been a slow night up until now and they were stoked on caffeine and sugar and were glad of the opportunity to investigate a disturbance.

Approaching the guys slowly, so as not to startle them and maybe wear a knife in the guts for just doing their jobs, the officers stopped a foot away from the group and watched Tash destroying Harri's shoe.

"Hey buddy, whaddya think you're doin'?" Officer Bob called.

As none of the guys were called Buddy they didn't even acknowledge the voice as it obviously wasn't addressing them. The guys continued to bitch amongst themselves about the time it was taking to get shit off a shoe and how urgent the need for a drink had become.

"I need a stick or something to dig the crap out of the tread," said Tash. "There's not much left now so find me something that's thin enough to use as a scraper."

"How about Sumo's impregnator," Phil offered helpfully.

"You're a real riot. And so original too," Sumo retorted.

Things were getting tense. They were on a buck's night - a night where everything was supposed to be amusing, no matter how juvenile, dangerous, stupid or unfunny it was. Instead, the guys were getting on each others tits.

"Fuckin' hurry up," Sumo screamed. "Who gives a fuck if he's got shit in his shoe. Who's gonna know?"

"Just give Harri his shoe back. He can finish the job off later," Marc said.

Officers Bob and Pete watched the guys getting pissed off. It was clear they weren't intentionally vandalising anything but a misdemeanour was still happening before their very pollution filled, blood shot eyes and swearing in a public place was bordering on obscene behaviour. Not only that, more than two people together on the streets at any one time automatically constituted a gang and gangs were notorious for being law breakers who held little regard for the life and limb of others. It was a paranoid society, for sure, but when you'd worked the beat for as long as Bob and Pete, and seen the things they'd seen, it paid to be suspicious of everyone - even your own mother. No one was above reproach.

"Hey buddy," Bob tried again, "whaddya think you're doin'?"

Again Tash and the guys ignored the voice.

Now, once could be excused as maybe not hearing the request owing to other noise, but twice was bordering on blatant ignorance. And Pete especially hated ignorance. His brother-in-law was ignorant and he detested him. He could feel his blood pressure rising and he hated when that happened because it made his haemorrhoids throb.

Taking a few steps closer, Pete took his nightstick out of his belt and poked Tash in the arm. Tash turned to face Pete and looked down at the stick that was still making contact.

"It's OK now," Tash said brightly, "I'm not gonna worry about digging the shit out, but thanks for the offer. Anyway, that stick looks too big. We needed a thin one to get in between the tread."

Tash handed the shoe back to Harri. "Let's go get us a drink."

Harri looked at the state of his shoe and couldn't believe how beat up it was. "Look what you did to my shoe, you heavy handed thug. Maybe I oughta get your head and knock the shit outta that. See how you like it. I can't wear this, it's destroyed."

"Yes you bloody can. Who cares about your fuckin' shoes. It's dark. Who's gonna see it. Let's go." Sumo was champing at the bit.

"You owe me a new pair of shoes you stinking, viral, toxic wind bag."

"Hey, I got most of the shit out didn't I, you ingrate. If we'd left it to you, you'd be missing half a leg by now. It's your fault for not looking where you walk." Tash looked at Officer Pete. "I said I didn't need the stick, so you can stop poking me with it now."

Pete stared hard at Tash. He didn't like his attitude. "Now you listen to me son, just calm down and we can settle this thing nicely."

"I am calm, and what thing?"

If Pete hadn't had his uniform on he would have hurt Tash, just because. But the law was the law and he would do the right thing because somehow he still believed in his job. He'd seen some of the other guys at the precinct turn into animals over next to nothing because they believed the uniform gave them the right, but he vowed to ask questions first, maim later. His nickname at the station was 'sanctimonious prick'.

Joc stepped forward. "Um Tash, you're talking to one of the local constables. Be nice." Joc smiled sweetly at Pete and stepped back.

Suddenly Tash looked worried. "Oh, I'm sorry. I didn't realise. I thought you were just another nutter. We've seen a few since we got here." Shit. Why did he say nutter? On Dectarus you could be arrested for saying that to a cop. On Dectarus, cops were revered. Tash started to fidget. The last thing he needed was an insubordination mark against his name. A police record followed you everywhere.

Pete eyed Tash suspiciously. There was something odd about him. "Your friend said I was a constable. In this city we're known as police officers. I take it you boys aren't from around here."

"That's right. We come from quite a way away," said Tash, very politely.

"England?"

England? Well they sort of had. "Yeah, that's right. We came here from England."

"I've never been there but I hear it's a nice place. You ever been there Bob?"

"Not me. I never even been out of the city." Bob was not an adventurous soul. That's why his wife was fat and depressed. She had nothing good to ever look forward to so she sat at home and involved herself in other people's lives via the wonderful world of television.

"So, why are you vandalising this post?" Pete asked.

"I wasn't vandalising it, const … er … police officer. I was using it to knock the shit out of Harri's shoe." Shit. Why did he say shit? Using foul language to a cop was another no-no. Beads of sweat sprang out above his top lip.

Pete could see he was making Tash nervous. If these guys had been from the city they would have had a brawl by now and arrested the lot of them, including their neighbours just for knowing 'em. Obviously the police in England were respected and feared, judging by Tash's reactions and the respectful silence of his mates. No one in this city cared anymore. The law was a joke and the cops were the butt of it. Maybe he'd see about a transfer. He liked the idea of being held in high esteem instead of being treated like a low-life piece of garbage for trying to keep the streets clean and people safe in their homes.

When he went off on these tangents of thought, Pete felt self-righteous and noble, like a great warrior who knew he could save the world if only he had a bit of help. As a show of good faith maybe he'd excuse Tash and his mates. He knew it was true what he'd said about the shoe and none of them had tried to run or threaten him and Bob with a gun or attempt to gouge their eyes out with a broken bottle. Now that was respect. Really, Pete couldn't be bothered with the paper work and the lawyers and the whole court system over a lousy post and a pile of doggy doo. It wasn't worth the overtime or the ink.

"Whaddya say Bob. We let these boys go? The post don't look any worse for wear an' I think they'll keep their noses clean from now on."

"Yeah, and our shoes, Harri piped up.

The guys laughed feebly at Harri's attempt at humour.

Pete was impressed by how nervous he made these guys. He knew they'd behave themselves. The crisp, clean, cold air in England obviously bred clean living people. Maybe that was the trouble with this city - the air. Maybe it stifled people and filled their bodies with toxins that mutated the goodness genes and turned them bad. That was a theory he just might look in to, when he had the time.

"OK, get movin'. An' don't let us catch ya' doin' anythin' wrong 'cos next time we might not be so nice. Enjoy your stay."

"Thanks. Thanks a lot. We'll go now and … and … we'll just go." Tash smiled his biggest, brightest smile and bowed at Bob and Pete as he backed away from the post. "Come on guys. Let's move."

They didn't need telling twice. They made off down the street at a marathon pace. Davis walked the quickest. He had enough adrenaline pumping through him to run the entire length of Manhattan Island and back again without stopping for a break. He was sweating more than Tash.

Bob and Pete watched them go and Pete addressed the small crowd. "OK people, break it up otherwise we'll arrest ya' for loitering."

"What a bunch of ghouls," said Bob. "Probably hopin' to see some blood."

"Yeah, ours." They turned away in disgust and went in search of their next caffeine and sugar fix. Bob was getting a withdrawal headache.

The crowd slowly dispersed. The majority of them were disappointed nothing had happened and that a camera crew hadn't shown up, just in case. It was the dream of most of these people to get their faces on TV and say something witty and clever like 'Hi Mom'. Little did they realise that in order to achieve their goal all they had to do was ring up Jerry Springer, tell him they were sexually attracted to a lesbian goat/their cross-dressing brother's block of cheddar/the neighbour's back fence, and an entire hour of abuse-filled airtime could have been theirs.

Sometimes the price of fifteen minutes of fame was just a bit too high.

Chapter 11

After speed walking for two blocks and not saying a word, the guys slowed their pace.

"Why do we get into trouble everywhere we go?" Joc asked. "We'll be banned from this place next, if we don't watch it."

"I thought for sure I was a goner," Tash said.

"You might still be. I think I've got a blister on my toe 'cos my shoe doesn't fit right and I strained my calf trying to keep it on my foot."

"You're breaking my heart," Tash said, not caring a single bit about Harri's newly developed limp. "They're bloody ugly shoes anyway. You should be thanking me; I improved the look of them."

"Just like my fist is gonna improve the look of your face."

"Settle down. Who gets this carried away over a pair of shoes? You gotta get a life."

Harri shut up. He couldn't be bothered arguing anymore and Tash was right. Anyone who placed as much emphasis on a pair of shoes, as he was doing, was definitely not having a fulfilling life.

"Drink, naked women, drink, drink. NOW!" Sumo declared forcefully. "We gotta stop fart-arsing around and do what we came here to do."

"Sumo's right. We gotta party 'til we can only see out of one eye," said Phil.

"Only twenty-seven more drinks," Sumo reminded them, "and the record is mine."

"So, where to?" Marc asked as he looked around to see if there was anything close to where they were. "We gotta see if Sumo's tough enough to last the distance. You know the last five are the hardest."

"Hey, I'm ready for it. I'm feeling good and I might not get another chance to try for it so nothin's gonna stop me. I'm gonna make it so no one ever beats my record. I'll drink anything you throw at me."

"Remember we're only four behind you. Except Kam, Tash and Marc who are trailing badly. They got no hope," Joc said.

"Those weak gutted wimps were never really in contention anyway. As for the rest of you, you'll be lucky to keep up."

Sumo's ego had a bad habit of running away with him when he'd had a few too many. He was so henpecked at home that the moment he got the chance to break free he quickly became full of self-importance and bravado. The guys let him have his few deluded moments of glory because they knew as soon as he got home he'd be humble again. Sotty was a force not to be reckoned with.

At one time or another each of them had been going for the title and each of them had bummed out in the closing stages of the game. They'd either peaked too early and collapsed in a pile of their own vomit or they'd tried to pace themselves and inadvertently gone over time.

It was a carefully monitored competition and even in their drunkest moments they each knew how much the others had drunk so no one could try and cheat and claim to have consumed more than they actually had. That was an offence immediately punishable by some kind of torture that usually involved wet towels and tweezers.

Sumo had three more hours in which to claim the much coveted trophy and judging by his physical condition (the fact that he was still standing upright and not flicking away imaginary bugs), he looked good to be a winner. But stronger men had failed before now and like Marc said, the last five drinks were the hardest.

"Come on you guys. This place is alive with activity. Surely we can find somewhere to have a drink where we won't be hassled for having fun," Phil said.

"Look, how about we follow a group of people and go where they're going. That's easy enough," Marc suggested.

"Sounds fair. How about that group over there," Joc said, pointing across the street.

"That's not a group, you idiot," Davis said, staring hard, "that's one man."

"No way," said Sumo, but Davis was right. "I tell you, I've seen some sights in my day but that must be the most viral."

"He needs a month on Fanstar. If the dysentery didn't get him the stomach parasites would. Maybe we could drop him off on our way back," Harri suggested helpfully.

"Nah, we'd never get the cruiser off the ground. It's got a maximum weight limit you know," Phil informed him.

"That reminds me of a joke," said Tash. "How do you lose a hundred and twenty kilos of ugly fat?"

"Dunno," they choroused.

"Get a divorce." They laughed. The party mood was coming back.

Scanning the streets for a real group of people who looked like they were going somewhere and not just loitering with intent, Kam thought he saw Sugar Anne.

"Guys, guys," he said excitedly, "it's her."

"Her who?" Joc asked.

"Sugar Anne."

"Where?" Sumo asked, looking around hoping to see the same as Kam. He looked left, right, up, down, but nowhere could he see a half naked woman. "You're delirious Kam. She ain't out here."

Kam pointed to a group of women. "There. The one in the blue jacket."

Sumo followed his finger. "That's not her," he said disappointed. "That's just someone with the same colour hair."

Kam looked harder to make doubly sure but Sumo was right. His heart broke for the second time that night. "Let's follow them anyway."

Hurrying to catch up to the women so they wouldn't lose sight of them, the guys pounded along the pavement making a lot of noise as they went. There were five girls in the group and if the guys had been New Yorkers they would have - one: never run up behind anyone as noisily as they were doing and actually hope to live; two: noticed the sudden lull in conversation between the girls; three: noticed the girls shoulders tense up as their footsteps got closer and; four: not assumed that girls were relatively harmless.

But like all good city people, the girls were armed with stun guns and mace and they were very adept at using their weapons so a group of potential muggers were no match for a group of women whose main aims were to have a good time in their own city without feeling constantly intimidated and scared. One little touch from the people behind and the girls would be on them so fast they wouldn't know what hit them. It paid to be prepared and prepared they were.

The guys knew they had no intention of hurting anyone but, unlike them, Earthlings weren't mind readers who enjoyed a comfortable state of existence, so everyone got treated as a potential criminal.

Laws on Dectarus were stricter, fairer and carried out as specifically expressed in the 'Decree of Harmful or Not', a small volume written by average citizens who believed in giving more than a slap on the wrist for sheer thuggery, anti-social behaviour and dishonesty in general.

With no way of twisting and interpreting the words and meanings of the laws to suit the criminals and their lawyers, especially to prolong a case beyond all reasonable limits and so drain the public purse and make one person rich in the process, the crime rate was low and people felt safe. Basically, criminals got what they deserved.

In the case of someone like Phil's old man, who made a few crooked deals here and there, it was deemed that because a lot of his dealings were done away from home, and as Dectarus still reaped the tax benefits from his profits, he wasn't thought of as a crim; just a fine citizen with a head for big business. Every now and then, when he'd pull a shonky deal at home, he'd justify his actions by giving small contributions to the 'Fight Whatever It Is We're Fighting For This Week' fund. To them, money was money, any way they came by it.

Overall, Dectarians were a less aggressive and nicer people anyway because they ate lots of green, leafy vegetables, smiled and waved at each other on the streets, wore only calming, soothing colours that were perfectly co-ordinated and brought out the best in their complexions and they never cut their fringes too short. Many of the other planets considered them to be the nerds of the solar system but secretly they envied their peace and orderliness. And as the guys proved, they still knew how to have a good time, so they weren't totally anal.

The guys were quite close to the girls now so rather than wait for a surprise attack the girls swung around and faced them. They stood with their hands on their hips and their attitudes on full show. The guys stopped dead and waited for them to turn around and continue on their way but they stayed put and faced the guys in defiance.

"Are you following us?" the tallest of the group asked. "'Cos if you are you'd better walk away now, in the opposite direction, and find someone else to bother. We ain't gonna take no shit from no one, especially not a bunch of losers like you. Do yourselves a favour and leave while you can still walk."

Oooh, tough talk. That kind of talk made Sumo nervous. She reminded him a bit too much of Sotty and he didn't like to have to think about her when she wasn't around and he certainly didn't wanna get into any sort of tangle with her because he knew from experience he'd come off second best.

Joc had hardly heard a word she'd said. He was more impressed by her long legs and dark, shiny hair. Her friends were pretty hot too. If they could lead him to a drink his life, at this moment in time, would be complete.

The other six stood there wondering why the girls were behaving in a hostile manner. Maybe a few chemical free veggies would help fix the problem. For a planet that was culturally similar to their own, the two were really nothing alike. Everyone here seemed to have a chip on their shoulder. They'd hardly encountered anyone friendly. Tash decided that if the day ever arrived when he was the buck, he was not going to come back here. Besides, the drinks were lousy and few and far between. He realised now that all the talk back home about why Earth was not a recommended destination were true.

The girls stood stock still, ready to reach for their protection at a single hint of trouble but the guys who stood before them weren't like your average muggers. They were nicely dressed - except the one in the white jumpsuit, they had a naïve look about them and they hadn't given the girls any lip. Normally they would have been called a load of choice names by now and told to stick their attitude where the sun don't shine.

"They might be tourists," the girl in the blue jacket whispered to Miss Legs. "Ask them."

"Like I care what they are," she said. Again she asked, "Are you following us?"

Sumo, who was well versed in the art of trying to placate an irritated woman, spoke up in a soothing manner. "We're looking for a bar and we're following you 'cos we thought you might be going to one."

"And what if we are? We don't like being followed so mind your own business and keep your distance."

Sumo looked at the guys and shrugged his shoulders. "It's just that we're on a ..."

"We don't care what you're on. Fuck off and stop following us."

With that, the girls turned around and carried on.

Well, that was that. Short, sharp and shiny. No niceties, no smiles, no friendly greetings. Herb and Pammy had been chummier, and they'd tried to mug them.

Not about to be deterred from getting another drink, the guys brushed aside the animosity - after all, they'd been spoken to worse than that before - and decided to follow the general direction the girls were taking anyway, but at a safe distance.

Walking slower and quieter, the guys trundled on. Why was it that when expectations for a night out were high the evening usually turned into a dud. They'd had some fun, for sure, but Marc wasn't getting into nearly as much trouble as he should have been, and that was the whole idea of the buck's night - to make the guy sorry he was leaving his mates behind in favour of a piece of skirt. Honestly, what could a woman give a man that his mates couldn't?

Even though the answer to that question was 'not much, apart from the obvious', not many people chose to stay single. Men and women were worlds apart in nearly all aspects of their being and still they had an urge to get together and torment the living shit out of each other for the better part of their lives. Maybe procreation had nothing to do with anything and the real desire of the cell was not to survive at all costs but to die a slow and painful death at the hands of a member of the opposite sex. Under the circumstances, this seemed the most logical explanation.

It didn't matter where you went in the entire system, the story was always the same. A few factors changed here and there but, all in all, incompatibility between the two genders was a universal thing; that is except on Unway and Frimter where they had five and twenty-seven different genders respectively. Life on Frimter was especially complicated and it was best not to use their 'Mail Order a Partner' service. A kinky Trobit had used the service as a last desperate measure to find true love, but her plans for happiness and really weird sex backfired when she received

'Version Nineteen: We know you didn't ask for this but it's all we've got left - please accept it with our apologies'.

Version Nineteen was capable of loving only itself and having sex with only itself, or Version Four in a pinch. The best the Trobit could hope for was a foot massage and a recital of Frimtian poetry which was renowned for its stories of frustration in attempting to find a perfect mate. The Trobit figured that any company was better than none and the foot massages alone were worth the postage to get the Frimter delivered to her door. All things considered, their lives turned out pretty well and they were voted 'The Happiest and Most Satisfied Couple' on Trobitus for six years running. Why they didn't win the seventh year is another story and one much too ugly and depraved to go into at this moment.

As the guys carried on it suddenly occurred to them they needed to take positive action right here, right now, so the party could get back into full swing. They decided they had two choices - go back to the cruiser and go somewhere else or give the city one more chance and find a bar, preferably with naked women.

The naked woman thing was a big pull to stay where they were.

"We do have one other choice," Tash said. "We could try and get another holographic disc to play on the cruiser. That would solve the woman problem until we got somewhere else."

"That's not a bad idea and maybe we could wrangle a shit load. Whaddya reckon?" Joc asked the others.

"I like it," said Sumo. About now he was ready to stick his head in a toilet bowl for a drink.

"So you wanna forget about finding another nightclub?" Marc asked.

"Yeah. Look for a disc shop instead. We can have better fun on the cruiser anyway," Phil said.

Kam was the only one who looked upset by the new arrangements. He knew the moment he stepped foot onto the cruiser Sugar Anne would be lost to him forever. He decided that the first thing he needed to do when he was back on board was have a B. Amber and Binzi Glow. If he couldn't be with her then he didn't want to remember that she even existed. He'd pine all the way back to the park and then let her go. He sighed heavily, resigned himself to his fate and thought of Sugar's thighs crushing his ribs, squeezing the life out of him. Love was definitely cruel.

Now that the guys had changed their plans, instead of finding a nightclub, they needed a disc shop.

Chapter 12

As luck would have it the guys chanced upon a disc store the very next corner they turned. For once something was working in their favour. The girls were long gone from their sights and the guys figured they'd be bad mouthing some other poor loser who'd made the mistake of being friendly. At least the holograms were friendly, and that's what the guys needed - a woman who was eager to please.

There was only a handful of people in the store but the number of discs available was more than the guys could have hoped for. Pictures of sexy women striking sexy poses adorned the walls. This was just the kind of shop Dectarus needed. Although holograms were popular on Dectarus you had to order them in from either Ellitas or Irtan.

The powers that be on Dectarus had decided that the only discs to be made available to its citizens were entertainment ones and then only in limited numbers. They reasoned that if people started to replace their partners with images they risked eventually dying out as a race. It was sound logic considering that Weezon was down to about five people and those remaining couldn't be bothered repopulating the place because they'd forgotten how and they'd gotten too comfortable living the high life with dead people's money.

The other planets didn't bother to intervene because Weezon had been full of corrupt officials who'd spent their lives cheating and robbing their trade partners of everything they could. A lot of them had even been known to sell their grandmothers for the right price. Not only that, they were horrifically and sickeningly ugly and as far as the other races were concerned they were a festering boil on the face of the universe.

The committee for 'Aesthetically Pleasing People, Places and Things' were not sorry to see them go because they always made the universe seem so untidy. To them the inventor of the holograms was worshipped as a Goddess to whom they regularly offered sacrifices of such things as vinyl shoes and tie-dyed T-shirts in eternal thanks for managing to eliminate a race of abominable creatures. Unsightly was unacceptable.

To say the guys were in awe was an understatement. They didn't know where to begin. There was much too much to choose from and they wanted the very best the city had to offer. Suddenly New York wasn't such a bad place.

While the guys stared at the posters, oohing and aahing at anything remotely resembling a female and a few things that didn't, Joc did the smart thing and approached the counter to get some much needed help. Standing quietly, assuming that the person working in the store would be only too happy to assist him as soon as he sensed his presence, Joc waited and waited while the guy chewed his gum noisily, flicked through a Rolling Stone magazine and hummed tunelessly to whatever it was that was playing way too loud for any normal person to bear.

"Excuse me," Joc said politely.

Slower than a snail stuck to dry cement the guy lifted his eyes to meet Joc's. Raising his right eyebrow he gave Joc the quick once over.

"Mmm," he said disinterestedly.

Joc had a sudden and all consuming urge to punch this guy straight in his worthless, sallow face. The only thing that stopped him were all the red and yellow lumps adorning the guy's skin. He obviously has some hideous disease and Joc was not going to contract it just for a moments satisfaction. Swallowing his fury at this guy's attitude, and knowing that he was about to rip him off blind, Joc asked for help.

"Can you recommend a good disc?"

The surly, acne-faced clerk, who really should have been working in a morgue, squinted his face into a most unbecoming look of 'Yeah, like I know what your tastes are and outta the thousands of artists available I'm gonna pick the exact one you love', said, "Maybe if I knew what ya' liked I could like maybe help you."

Hey, don't crack a sweat for me pal, thought Joc.

"OK, we want a really hot woman who likes to get down and get dirty and who's a really hot dancer. Clothes are a definite option and she's gotta have a great body that she doesn't mind sharing and we don't care if she goes solo or does group scenes."

This guy didn't want a music store he wanted a brothel. Because his thought processes were minimal and his mind didn't like to over-exert itself, he automatically recommended the woman he'd been force-fed as a child. "You want Madonna."

Without waiting to see if Joc needed further assistance he re-focused his attention on his magazine and took up his chewing where he'd left off.

"And where do I find Madonna?" Joc asked the festering sack of pus irritably.

Duh. "Under 'M'," he said, "for moron," he muttered.

Joc re-joined the others. "Everybody look for Madonna. She's supposed to be hot."

The discs were sorted into various diverse categories such as Jazz, Rock and Classical. Each of the guys took a different musical genre and looked under 'M'. The order booklets back home didn't set the discs out as elaborately as this. Mind you, the selection wasn't quite as huge either. Harri thought it was interesting how the discs had been separated according to music type. The music was fairly inconsequential really, in comparison to the action.

Marc, who had been assigned the 'Contemporary' section, found their goddess. "I've got her," he shouted excitedly.

Kam was the only one who didn't run to him. He was secretly looking for Sugar Anne's name. He desperately hoped she was on disc. So far, no luck. He did come across a Dolly Parton though and he knew the guys would be interested in her. He grabbed the disc out of the rack, finished flicking through the 'Country and Western' section and went to shows the guys his find.

Ogling Madonna on the disc suggestively titled 'Like a Virgin', the guys knew they had come to the right place and when Kam held up Dolly for the guys to see they were beside themselves with ecstatic delight. Obviously Madonna was not the only woman who had something to offer.

The guys took charge of several racks each and sorted through the other letters. Right before their hungry eyes lay a veritable smorgasbord of hot women.

Harri picked out Olivia Newton-John in 'Totally Hot', and he bet she was, while Sumo went back to the 'Country and Western' section in search of more Dolly Parton or women similar to her. He figured that anyone who called their disc 'Here You Come Again' was bound to be popular and have plenty more titles to choose from.

The guys were making such a ruckus yelling to each other when they'd struck gold that zit boy actually looked up to check out what was going on. "Hey, are yous gonna buy somethin' or what?"

Joc looked over at him. "Don't get viral. We're still choosing."

Viral? Zitty shrugged and let them get on with it. All the discs were security protected so they weren't likely to try and steal anything. And what did he care if the guys were noisy? He earned a lousy five bucks an hour for working his butt off, making someone else rich. Capitalism was a wonderful thing - if you were the one banking the money and not the one being exploited. He put his head back down and got on with the difficult business of reading about what the rich and famous were up to.

By the time the guys had finished choosing the sexiest looking women, whose discs had titles that promised a good time, they had fifty discs between them. They were eager to get back to the cruiser and put them on but the hard part was going to be smuggling them out without calling attention to themselves.

"How about if we put them inside Marc's suit. Most of them will fit into the inside pockets and the rest can go down the legs and arms. It'll block the anti-theft protection device and we'll be outta here in no time."

"Good thinking, Phil," Joc said.

As nonchalantly as they could, the guys started slipping the discs into the suit. Luckily the clerk was completely uninterested in anything that was going on inside the store otherwise he would have seen straight away what was happening. Even the handful of browsers couldn't have cared less about what the guys were up to.

Smuggling fifty discs was no mean feat. The corners of the cases were poking into Marc's thighs and arms, he looked about fifteen kilos heavier than when he walked in and his movements were now severely restricted.

"You guys start walking out and I'll pretend I'm gonna buy something so we don't look suspicious. Give me a disc and I'll distract pus face," said Joc.

Joc strolled casually back to the counter while the others made their way back to the doors. Marc looked like a stiff robot from a bad sci-fi movie because he was moving slowly with his arms and legs unnaturally wide apart. They had better be worth the trouble, he thought, and he hoped the suit would block the anti-theft device because there was no way he'd be able to make a quick get away if the thing went off.

Joc laid the disc down on the counter quietly. He figured that by the time Mr. Ignorant decided to serve him the guys would be out of the store. Joc stood very still while Billy placed a bookmarker in his magazine, closed it slowly and put it down.

"You find what ya' want?" Like I care, he thought.

"I hope so. Is this a good one?" Joc asked, pointing at the disc.

Billy rolled his eyes contemptuously. "The Mormon Tabernacle Choir. Yeah, great. That'll be nineteen ninety-five."

"Nineteen ninety-five what?"

This guy is such a loser, thought Billy. "Dollars man, what else?"

"Dollars. Right. Um, I don't think I got that many." Joc surreptitiously glanced at the door. The guys had made their escape without so much as a beep. It was safe for Joc to leave. "I'll have to pass on this then. Well, thanks anyway."

Billy shrugged his shoulders. "Whatever." If there was one thing he couldn't stand it was idiots like this guy coming in and disturbing his reading time for big, fat nothing. Friendly chit-chat without any cash forthcoming at the end of it was a waste of breath and brain power as far as he was concerned. Was it that he looked like such a nice, accommodating guy people thought he was there purely for their benefit? In future he'd try to be less friendly and helpful then maybe they'd leave him alone so he could get on with his own thing. He'd given up smiling the day he'd turned sixteen, now it was time to give up everything he'd been taught about customer relations. He felt released. Who said puberty was a difficult time?

Back out onto the safety of the street, Joc looked around for the guys. They were gone! It was like they'd disappeared into thin air. He did a complete circle but he couldn't see them anywhere. Those bastards had deserted him.

"Psst, Joc. Over here," Phil hissed.

Joc looked around again. He couldn't tell where the voice was coming from. "Where are you?" he whispered loudly.

"Walk straight ahead and around the corner."

Joc did as instructed. In the dark shadows of an alley way stood his group of criminal friends.

"I thought you bastards had done a runner. We ready to head back now? I gotta see this Madonna."

"We need a bag or something to put the discs in," Tash said. "Kam left the knapsack at the club and Marc can hardly move. Go back in the store and ask the guy for one."

"No way. If he smiled he'd hurt himself. You go Kam. He might give you one."

"OK."

Dutifully, Kam walked around the corner and back into the store. Standing at the counter being totally ignored for what seemed like an eternity he finally spoke. "Hey, am I invisible."

"Are you buyin' anythin'?"

"No."

"Then you're invisible."

"Look, I was wondering, could I just have a bag please?"

"Are you buyin' anythin'?"

"I already said no."

"Then ya' can't have a bag. What do I look like - a convenience store? No freebies 'round here pal."

"How much does a bag cost?"

"I dunno. How much ya' got?"

"Nothing."

"Well nothin' equals no bag. Comprende?"

Kam walked back to the guys empty handed. "He wouldn't give me one."

"Shit. What'll we do?" Marc asked.

"How about we divide them up between us," Kam offered.

The guys looked at each other. How bloody simple was that? They couldn't believe it hadn't occurred to them.

"How'd you come up with something so logical?" Sumo asked Kam. "That's almost a flash of brilliance."

"I don't know."

"Earth's atmosphere must agree with you. Since your accident you've hardly said anything sensible. Maybe you should stay here." Joc said.

Kam's eyes took on a dreamy stare. He would love to stay and live happily ever after with his Sugar Anne.

"Hello. Could we hurry up and divide our booty. I'm getting jabbed and poked from all sides here." Marc was getting annoyed because they were just standing there marvelling at Kam's one brainy moment.

"OK. Give us six each and you keep eight," Phil said. "You got the most pockets."

Reaching inside the suit Marc pulled out several discs at a time and handed them around. It felt good to be rid of them. "What a relief," he said as he scratched and rubbed his torso.

When he started bending and stretching and generally overdoing the whole relief thing, a sudden and intense urge to gouge Marc's eyes out swept over Sumo. He kept relatively calm, however, because a set of gouged and bleeding eyes would, naturally enough, require some kind of medical treatment. Such treatment would take up precious viewing time and Dolly, whom he was itching to see and feel, deserved not to be kept waiting. Therefore he would speak; not maim.

"Are you quite done with all the piss fartin' around?" Sumo asked pointedly. He was trying hard to disguise the impatience in his voice. "Can we move it out now?"

Marc finished off with a couple of knee bends. "Ready when you are. Lead the way."

But instead of moving off they stayed put, looking at each other expectantly.

Phil cleared his throat and voiced what they were all thinking. "Umm, does anyone remember how to get to the park?"

No one said anything. Although the guys had virtually walked in a straight line from the park, they had crossed a couple of roads, turned a couple of corners, had a few more drinks and seen a bit of trouble since they left the cruiser. All of the night's excitement had left them a bit disoriented. None of them knew where they were or how to get back.

"We'll haffta ask someone the way," Joc said.

"Are you gonna ask? I'm frightened to talk to anyone 'round here. All you get is a lot of aggro and nothing else," said Tash.

"All someone has to do is point us in the general direction. How hard can that be?" Sumo said. "I'll ask. Let's move out onto the street and find someone."

Stepping out of the shadows the guys could have easily been mistaken for a bunch of thugs who hung around back alleys waiting for some poor drunk to come by so they could roll him. They weren't to know that the protocol in a big city was to never emerge from a dark place and then expect to be treated with any degree of civility by the paranoid and wary residents.

People who saw them emerge from the alley rapidly crossed the street. Others stopped mid stride, did an about face and headed back in the direction from which they'd just come. Watching everyone scurry in different directions was like watching a bunch of rats abandoning a sinking ship. This was not good. No one was game enough to come near the guys. How were they supposed to get directions now?

"Why is everyone avoiding us like we got the dreaded Swampliner Flu?" Sumo wanted to know.

"Who knows anything about anything around here. Well, I for one don't care anymore. I'm gonna walk up to that guy with the stripy hat and ask him where the fucking park is and I don't give a shit if he abuses me for asking." Joc was as irritable as all hell and when he used the 'F' word the others knew he was not a happy chappy. He may have been a bastard, but he was polite.

Being a man on a mission, Joc crossed the road and virtually charged the stranger. When he was practically upon him he stopped. "Hey, which way's the park?"

Completely unconcerned by Joc's threatening stance and tone of voice, the odd looking guy said, "In this city we use manners when speaking to a stranger; now ask nicely or I won't tell you."

"Excuse me? No one around here is even remotely polite so don't give me that manners shit. Where's the park?"

"Tut, tut. Say the magic word."

This weirdo had Joc by the short and curlies, one: because Joc refused to use his telepathy and go anywhere near this guy's mind and two: he was the only visible person left on the street. Why did Joc have to accost the one human who insisted on manners? Talk about bad luck. "Which way is it to the park, please?" he asked through gritted teeth.

"That's better. See how easy it is to be polite? People would achieve so much more if they used a few manners. Don't you feel so much closer to God now?"

"Whatever you say," Joc sighed.

"Do you want Battery Park or Central Park?"

"Central."

"Now, let's see. If you go that way… no wait, it's that way. Or is it that way…" he mumbled, pointing in the opposite direction for the second time and looking very unsure. "OK, I've got it now. You want to go uptown."

Well, that's a big help. I don't know why I needed to ask. Just go uptown. It's that easy. As much as it irked him, he kept his thoughts to himself. "And which way would that be?"

Silence.

"Please." Smug bastard.

"Walk straight ahead that way and you'll come out in the general vicinity. Thank you, and have a nice night. I'll include you in my prayers, brother. God has always got room for one more wayward soul."

Without saying anything more, Joc headed back to the guys. "What an absolute loon. He's definitely the last person I'm talking to; this city is way too scary for me. He reckons the park's that way and I hope he's right. Let's just get outta here."

They didn't need to be told twice. The guys had been to plenty of places and seen plenty of things. In all reality, New York City was actually no better or worse than anywhere else, except for Qwol - which was tetrally awesome and Wigfeel - which was a viral dump.

It was just that expectations were so high for a good night out that every little misfortune or semblance of strange behaviour was magnified ten-fold. When they looked back on Marc's buck's night they would probably remember New York with a greater fondness than they felt for it right now. Another drink and another naked woman would make everything seem OK. They needed so little in their lives to keep them happy.

Chapter 13

Having gone so long without a drink had nearly sobered the guys up. Fortunately they had enough alcohol coursing through their systems to keep their livers occupied for a while yet, but the object was to drink until your internals were on the verge of suicide. When they got back on the cruiser they decided they'd push themselves to the very limits. They had to - it was the principle of the thing.

As they moved further up the street the familiar hustle and bustle of activity surrounded them again. The quietness they'd just left behind had been unnaturally eerie. They were glad to have the company of strangers again but nothing on the stretch of pavement was recognisable.

"You sure this is the right way?" Harri asked. "I don't recognise anything."

"It'd better be. If we go along a couple of those streets we might get back to where we started," Joc said, pointing to the streets that ran horizontally.

"Yeah, but which way. Left or right?" Phil said.

"This is a nightmare," said Marc. "We're gonna haffta ask again." From where he stood, Marc suddenly shouted. "Excuse me. Anyone. Hello. Are we heading the right way for the park?"

"Central Park," Joc added quickly.

Five sets of eyes looked at the guys.

"What's your problem, man?" a guy with too many fake gold chains around his neck asked Marc as he slowly approached.

"We wanna know if we're heading the right way for Central Park?"

"You mean ya' don't know? D'ya hear that Sol," he said to the guy a few paces behind him, "they want directions 'cos they're lost. Aaah. And what do I get for my trouble in helpin' you babies find your way back to mommy?"

"Um, a thank you," said Harri stupidly, not getting Lennie's gist.

"You're crackin' me up man. I meant somethin' more valuable; somethin' more worthy of my expertise that you are seekin'."

Clearly nothing came free in this city unless you struck upon someone who was trying to change the world for the better. What a piss ant situation this was. They seemed to be going from bad to worse.

"Forget it, we'll find our own way. Come on guys, just keep moving." Joc noticed that this guy had the same disease on his face as the one in the disc shop. Obviously it was contagious.

"Whatever ya' say man. But if ya' keep walkin' this way ya' might not get where ya' wanna go. For a small token of appreciation I could set you straight right here an' now." Lennie checked out his fingernails as he spoke.

Joc fiddled behind his ear, turned his switch on and honed in on Lennie's thoughts.

"OK guys, I got it. If we keep heading straight and turn left on Fifty Ninth, we'll be right there."

Lennie eyed Joc suspiciously. "How'd you suddenly know that?"

"You told me Lennie, that's how."

"No I didn't."

"Yeah you did," said Sumo.

"Loud and clear," said Marc.

Lennie was confused. Joc had said exactly what he'd been thinking and he knew his name too. He must have opened his mouth. Damn, he'd never be any good at this extortion game if he kept blabbin' information for free, 'cept he couldn't remember sayin' anythin'. Nah, he hadn't spoken. "Are you messin' with my head?"

"Ssh, can you hear that? I think your mama is calling you home Lennie. Seems you're up way past your bedtime and she doesn't sound happy. You'd better run off home now," Joc teased.

Lennie listened. It was true. He could hear a shrill voice telling him to get his scrawny, sorry ass home this second. Man, his mother could yell loud, but it was like she was inside his head. This was spooky. Lennie's right eye started to twitch and he nibbled nervously on his nails. He'd better go or else he'd be in for it in the morning. He couldn't wait for the day he turned twenty-one, then he could stay out all night rippin' people off if he wanted.

Worse still was the fact that if this guy could hear his mother, then his mates would be able to as well. He looked at the group of under age drinkers and smokers who were his friends. They were busy talking amongst themselves about which brand of cigarettes was most likely to tear your throat up first. As far as Lennie could tell, they were unaware of a nagging, grating voice wafting on the breeze. He afforded himself a bit of relief at that, but he was feeling queasy.

Joc had tapped into Lennie's greatest fear - his mother. He couldn't be bothered delving any further than that. He'd scared him enough for one night.

"I'm goin' home," Lennie said to his friends, "'cos my mom wants me to." Lennie furrowed his brow. He hadn't meant to say that. That wasn't tough. Shit.

"When ya' get out of diapers, come back," Sol said and everyone laughed.

Lennie was as good as rejected from the gang and he'd worked so hard for respect. It'd be a while before he could show his face around these parts again. He put his hands in his pockets, hung his head and slunk away around the corner. His 'friends' didn't even watch him go.

"Hey Sol," Joc called as the guys started moving off, "you're gonna haffta go home and masturbate again tonight because Helen ain't never gonna have sex with you. She thinks you're a real loser. Besides, she's screwing Kyle. She keeps you hanging 'cos Kyle only screws her when Courtney won't put out and she figures it's better to have someone than no one. Have a nice night now, boys and girls."

The guys strolled away casually. Kyle, Courtney, Sol and Helen stared at each other open mouthed. Was that guy a clairvoyant, or what? Just before the guys got out of hearing range it began. Punches were thrown, shirts were ripped, skin was scratched and hair was pulled out of heads.

"That'll keep them amused for awhile," Joc said, "and Lennie will suddenly be a good friend again in the morning."

"You're a real mender of broken hearts, Joc," Tash said, batting his eyes. "You make me feel so warm and fuzzy inside."

"Hey, everyone deserves a friend like me."

The closer they got to Central Park, the more their mood began to pick up. Knowing where they were going helped as well. They finally got to Fifty Ninth after a brisk walk of about fifteen minutes. The city hadn't slowed down much and traffic was still heavy. The most important thing now, besides getting back onto the cruiser, was getting a few quick drinks down them.

Marc knew how lucky he was they'd come to New York City and had a hard time of things. Had they gone anywhere else he would have been subjected to an endless barrage of torment and dangerous stunts that would have left him with a bit more than a mono-brow and the memory of a wild ride on an unstable chair. For him, at least, the night had been a good one. But as he was aware - the night wasn't over yet and because of the way things had gone, he could be in for worse. He really, really hoped not.

000 128 000

Entering the park at the same point they'd exited, the guys headed in a straight line down the path. Coming into the park straight off the busy streets made the place seem a bit spooky and strangely quiet. Not a single star could be seen in the night sky because of low cloud and smog cover. The beauty of thousands of other homes were lost to the people because the filth produced by mechanisation had cut them off from the rest of the universe. It was no wonder Earthlings didn't travel too far - they hadn't figured out how to break through the thick, dirty atmosphere cheaply and economically yet without creating more choking fumes in the process.

The only sound in the Park was the sound of the guys' footsteps and Tash's stomach. It gurgled and growled and built up a cache of gas ready for later use. To the others the sounds were not welcome, even if they did live by the adage that if they didn't have bodily functions to keep them amused, they'd have nothing.

"I wonder if Herbie and Pammy are still hanging 'round?" Harri said, looking around and trying to see through the darkness ahead.

"The tourist commission oughta put them on the pay-roll," Marc laughed.

"Yeah, they were good entertainment," agreed Sumo.

"We encountered all sorts tonight," said Joc. "Hope this trip doesn't give me nightmares."

"We've seen worse," Phil reminded.

They couldn't disagree.

They walked on unheeded. It was cold but there wasn't a breath of wind. The trees were perfectly still and all of nature was asleep for the night. It was like the Park was abandoned and the guys were glad because they didn't feel like dealing with anyone else tonight.

"Are we going anywhere else or just heading home?" Marc asked.

"The cruiser has to be at the Stardust at four o'clock. It'll take about thirty-five minutes, at an easy pace, to get home. I figure we got about fifty minutes to play because it's better if we arrive a coupla minutes early. You know how temperamental E.P. gets if you're late," said Joc.

"He's an artist, he's allowed to be moody," Sumo defended. He only said that because he fancied himself as a bit of a poet. But only in his private moments.

"We still got drinking time at the Stardust while we wait for the repairs," reminded Phil.

"Well, the best thing to do is cruise around, watch the discs and drink our way into the record books," said Marc. He hoped the suggestion would keep him safe.

That settled it. They had a firm plan and it was a good one because it involved booze and women.

"So, which bunch of trees is the cruiser parked behind?" Sumo asked Phil. "Everything looks the same."

Phil was rubbing his chin and looking around. "I think there's some yellow and purple flowers near the spot. Did anyone else notice any landmarks?"

They shrugged.

"If we get desperate I'll use the auto control on the key ring and have the cruiser meet us."

"Why doncha just use it anyway?" Harri asked. "It'll save messing around."

"'Cos last time I used it the cruiser took off and didn't return for an hour because of a malfunction in the signal receiver chip." Phil furrowed his brow and looked mildly irritated at the memory.

The wayward cruiser had decided that the music coming from a party on the habitable side of Hijin was calling to it, not its auto control signal. Phil knew this because when it returned it brought with it two drunken love birds having wild sex in the bathroom. They thought they were still at the party and were most put out that Phil dared to interrupt their session to inform them otherwise. Politely, he told them to carry on and whisked them home again. Rather rudely, they didn't thank him nor invite him in for a drink. From that moment on, Phil determined he would never act as a taxi service again. Unless it was for a girl, who was alone, and preferably naked.

Carrying on, they looked for coloured flowers. There weren't any. Phil deviated off the path and into the bushes. The cruiser was not there. The thing was so big so it wasn't like it could be easily overlooked. Maybe it was further up than he realised. "Keep walking," he said as he emerged from the greenery.

They walked a little further, wandered amongst a few more bushes and came away a little more uncertain each time.

"Mmm. I don't think we started this far up the Park. The walk to the road wasn't this long, was it?" Phil said.

"Nup. Maybe it's been stolen," Joc said. They would be well and truly stuffed if it had. Nothing on this Earth could possibly get them home in half an hour. That was not a good thought.

"Let's walk back amongst the trees," Marc suggested.

"I don't see how we can miss the thing. Let's face it, it sticks out like a Phallian's balls." Harri was not helping the situation. His words made Phil nervous because they were true.

Kam's mind - what was there of it - was still on Sugar Anne. He secretly hoped they never found the cruiser then he'd be stuck here for all eternity and he'd spend his life worshipping the very ground his love walked upon. He sighed a lovesick sigh.

Phil snapped his fingers and stopped walking. "Of course. That's it."

"What's it?" Marc asked.

"The cruiser. It's not there because it's not there."

"I think we figured that out, otherwise we'd all be aboard getting oiled," Sumo snapped.

"Nah, what I mean is, it's not there but it's there."

"Someone slap him 'til he makes some sense please," Marc said.

"Let me." Sumo strode towards Phil.

"If you'll let me finish …" Phil said irritably. "The cruiser must've rendered itself invisible. The old man must've fitted the new 'Try Stealing This Now, Punk' anti-theft device. I reckon someone tampered with the cruiser and set the thing off. It's a 'now you see it, now you don't' type but not like the old 'Warp Forward'."

"That death trap. Well at least the cruiser won't suddenly land on us," Davis said, relieved.

Chapter 14

In its time, the 'Warp Forward' was the brightest and most innovative idea to hit the west side of the system in years. Vehicle theft had been on the increase for some time and nothing anyone did to protect their property from marauding thieves was working. For every type of alarm or kill switch or locking device that came onto the market a counter device was almost immediately discovered. High tech theft was fast becoming the career of the future. But one small company on Wayfare managed to change all that.

After a particularly hard day at the office, and a blistering fight with his juvenile delinquent son, Mr. Forward, of the Advance Forward Company, was not in a good mood when he left work for the night. On top of that his wife had organised for them to go to yet another boring cocktail party at the Baton-Smuts on the neighbouring planet of Omin and he didn't feel like flying all the way there to put up with the obnoxious couple and their friends.

Walking around the side of the building and into the parking lot he noticed it was completely empty. That would have been OK if he hadn't been standing there but as he was still there, and not at home, it wasn't OK because it meant his vehicle was missing; stolen, yet. Now stolen shouldn't have been so unusual except that Mr. Forward was the leader in anti-theft devices. He continually bragged that nothing of his ever got nicked. Ha! Well now something had. He doubted if anyone would have any sympathy.

His all singing, all dancing, state-of-the-art, brand spanking new machine had gone. He'd taken it straight off the production line seven days earlier, had it especially painted to match his eyes - which many considered a big mistake because they were a murky brown colour - and personally fitted the very latest 'Don't Touch Or You'll Lose Your Fingers' laser alarm. As there were no stray fingers hanging around the general vicinity of where his vehicle should have been, it was pretty obvious that the device had not lived up to its name.

Standing all alone in the empty parking lot he wondered how he was going to get home. Then he realised he couldn't go to the party now because he had no way of getting there. For the first time that day he smiled. Taking his communication screen out of his case he called the car theft division of the local retrieval establishment. There was no point in calling the police because they'd handed the car theft division over to a private family business years ago. For a small insurance fee each year the family did their best to get your property back. Most of the time they were successful. It seemed that only the rarest or most valuable vehicles never got recovered.

Rumour had it the family organised the thefts in the first place, held onto the vehicle for a few days and miraculously spotted it in some way off place after lapsed premiums had been paid up, with a little extra on top for patience and understanding. No one could prove this, of course, not that anyone wanted to anyway because the family were highly volatile if rubbed the wrong way and trying to own anything of value ever again would be a wasted effort because it would be stolen within hours of receipt, never to be seen again.

So, Mr. Forward called the family Colletti and told them of his trouble. After much irritation in trying to convince them his fees had been paid and that he didn't need to transfer any more funds, the second set of books revealed that he was in fact financial and consequently they would tend to his needs at once. The boss, Mr. Ron as he liked to be called, apologised for the accusation and the inconvenience Mr. Forward found himself in and offered to send his son to pick him up and deliver him to his home. This was gratefully accepted.

Mr. Forward was promised that his vehicle would be speedily located and returned forthwith, hopefully before business the following day. Mr. Forward said this suited him fine because there was a particular function that evening he didn't want to attend. Mr. Ron understood perfectly. He too was married.

Mr. Forward then called his wife and told her what had happened. He said Steev - the youngest Colletti - would be bringing him home shortly. Mrs. Forward was not pleased that she'd bought a very expensive dress for a party she couldn't go to and suggested they hire a Galabus for the evening. Mr. Forward tried to look and sound enthused by her idea and said that if he was home in time they would most certainly still go. He smiled sweetly at her through the screen and for the first time noticed that she had a crooked nose. He signed off and waited.

While he waited for Steev he thought there had to be an anti-theft device that was completely foolproof. He hated being at the mercy of others and he hated that his existing device was useless - although he liked the timing of the thieves. Then, what started as a vague, wishful thought suddenly set itself off in his head - like a bomb exploding. He had wished he could make his vehicle invisible at will and then no one would be able to see it to steal it. And that was it. That was how he came up with the super-dooper plan for the 'Warp Forward'.

It was so simple he wondered why he hadn't thought of it before. Probably because he'd never needed it before, he realised. And as long as there were crooks there was a need for his devices. It was thieves who kept him in business. But this 'Warp Forward' could make him the richest man on the entire planet of Wayfare and then he could retire in absolute, unadulterated luxury. Yes, he liked the idea and he figured if he cut the family Colletti in for a percent of the nett they wouldn't object too strongly to his plan. He didn't want to take any business away from them. It probably wasn't in his best interests to anyway.

Just as he was thinking of the Colletti's, Steev arrived. If he went home straight away he'd still be in time for the party and that was no good. So, with his idea fresh in his head he suggested to Steev that he not be taken home immediately but, instead, taken to see Mr. Ron to talk some business. Steev contacted his father and Mr. Ron agreed to talk to Mr. Forward when he heard there was possible profit in it for him. Mrs. Forward could wait a little while longer. He'd blame his lateness on Steev, saying he took his time in picking him up.

Mr. Forward and Mr. Ron had a very productive meeting indeed. Mr. Forward chose his words very carefully when he talked about the high rate of theft in the community and how secretly he appreciated the extra business his company turned over when things constantly went missing. However, he had an idea for an anti-theft device that would be a sure-fire way of guaranteeing the security of one's vehicle. Naturally, he added, not everyone would be able to afford such a device so theft was still bound to happen. Mr. Ron visibly relaxed when this fact was pointed out.

Mr. Forward explained to Mr. Ron that in the interests of his insurance business, which was kept going by the continued ease of theft, he had come to him - as a fellow businessman - to see if he would be interested in putting a small sum of money towards the project and taking a percent of the profits they were bound to make. He had no intention of doing anyone out of business and he had no intention of making any enemies and that is why he felt the Colletti family would make suitable partners.

The idea for the 'Warp Forward' was that the owner, upon exiting their vehicle, would set a timer that indicated when the owner would be returning to said vehicle. Once set, the vehicle would disappear. But it didn't just go invisible it actually warped forward in time and arrived back at its parking spot at the time indicated by the owner. The beauty of the device was that, because the vehicle wasn't there, it couldn't be stolen. It was brilliant and simple to achieve.

Mr. Ron considered the plan carefully and decided there was money to be made in such an idea. He agreed to the partnership and Mr. Forward was very happy. Steev took him home and Mrs. Forward was very unhappy. She threw a large stone pot at her husband and stormed around the house making noises about how her social opportunities were slim enough without him stuffing them up further.

Mr. Forward told his wife how they would soon be very, very rich and then she was very happy. She would be the one holding the cocktail parties. People would be coming to her. She picked up the pieces of the broken pot and brushed the stone dust from her husband's jacket.

'Warp Forward's' were churned out and fitted to all manner of vehicles. The money was pouring in. There were a few minor drawbacks in the plan though that, surprisingly, no one thought of until they happened. Because parking spaces appeared to be empty, vehicles would naturally pull in and their unsuspecting owners would go off and do their shopping or their business confident in the fact their vehicle would be waiting for them when they returned.

However, in several freak occurrences, warp forward times had been set for the exact same moment and so two or more vehicles would suddenly materialise together. And together they would stay - melded forever in a hideous tangle that some would have considered worthy of being called Modern Art.

Most owners got over this when they were duly compensated for their loss and Mr. Forward lost a bit of money but not enough to concern him greatly. He devised a simple solution to the parking problem - a small sign indicating that the space was occupied at the present and so would the person desiring to park please go elsewhere. The Colletti's made sure none of the signs were ever stolen. People were happy.

It wasn't until a group of holidaying Nampereons, using a hire van to get around in, arrived back a couple of minutes earlier than their set time and stood waiting for their vehicle within the confines of the parking space instead of off to the side, as would be the sensible thing to do. Consequently the van arrived right on time and landed on top of them wiping out the entire family except for the Grandmother who had stopped to have a quick look at some good luck beads. Deciding not to buy any, because she thought she was getting ripped off, she turned around just in time to see her only surviving relatives become horribly enmeshed within the metal of the van. Because none of them knew what had hit them, death was quick and painless.

Granny's first thought was to sue. It was a natural reaction that had been genetically engineered into her race many generations ago. And sue she did; not only Mr. Forward but the bead seller as well because it was her fault she hadn't been killed along with the rest of her family. If the bead seller hadn't been in the spot she was, Grandma wouldn't have stopped in the first place or, if her wares hadn't been too expensive, Grandma may have purchased something and the beads - being good luck ones - may have helped to avert certain disaster.

She hired a Nampereon lawyer because they had the dubious reputation of being the most ruthless and unscrupulous types you could find anywhere and they knew how to bleed everyone, who was within a ten mile radius of the accident, dry. They were good - no doubt about it.

Mr. Forward and the hapless bead seller lost everything. To add insult to injury, it was during one of his wife's many cocktail parties that Granny and her 'people' arrived unexpectedly, muscled in and took every last piece of furniture from under everyone's noses. Mrs. Forward was highly embarrassed and ran around apologising profusely to her guests as glasses were ripped out of their hands and taken away never to be seen again. Grandma even took their son - which actually wasn't as distressing as the Forward's thought it would be.

Because of the huge press the case got and the usual one-sided, highly biased reporting that went with such circuses, anyone who had had a 'Warp Forward' fitted to their vehicle panicked unnecessarily and had it removed and returned to more conventional means of anti-theft security.

The Colletti's managed to avoid legal action because they were silent partners in the 'Warp Forward' deal - for tax reasons, of course - and so they only lost the extra income but now vehicle theft was more rife than ever so they continued to do very well for themselves.

Mr. Forward and his shamed wife left Wayfare and moved to the small, out of the way planet Ertia. They changed their names and, the now, Mr. And Mrs. Lostall went into business again. This time Mr. Lostall invented an anti-theft device that simply rendered the vehicle invisible if it was tampered with in any way. This made theft and getting parking tickets impossible and there was no risk of being swallowed up by your vehicle should you be stupid enough to be standing in its return path.

A simple beam emitted from your key ring saw the vehicle instantly materialise before your eyes. It was a no-risk gadget that promised, and delivered, one hundred percent security. A small red light was the only thing that remained visible to indicate that the parking spot was taken so unnecessary collisions could be avoided. The Lostall's didn't feel like being sued again.

The 'Try Stealing This Now, Punk' made millions.

Phil's old man didn't contribute to those millions because he got his from a friend of a friend who knew someone in the business.

Chapter 15

Phil dug in his pockets for the keys. Nothing. He patted himself down. Nothing. He frowned. "Have one of you guys got the keys?" he asked, with a hint of panic in his voice.

"Please!" Marc rolled his eyes. "Just get the cruiser back; we all need a drink."

"I lost the keys." Eyes wide as if to suggest panic and fear.

"I don't think so. Stop piss fartin' around."

Sumo gave Phil a 'if I'm missing naked women because of you, you're gonna get hurt' look. Phil quickly dropped the performance. "How'd ya know I was faking?"

"You can't act for shit. You could get a job on that really viral show - 'My Life And Yours'."

"That's a good show," said Sumo.

"I should've known you'd watch it," Marc said distastefully. "It's badly dubbed and cheap and nasty. It should be called - 'I've Known You For Five Minutes So Now I Can Totally Interfere In Your Life, Sleep With Your Family, Get Caught, Get Killed and Miraculously and Inexplicably Come Back Six Months Later With a New Face and a Nastier Personality Than Before, Cause Nothing But Trouble and Bankrupt You Before You Realise I'm Not Really a Friend At All'," Marc said.

The others avoided looking at Marc for a moment and were unusually quiet, neither agreeing with him nor disagreeing with Sumo. Obviously they were closet viewers.

Phil pulled the keys out of his shirt pocket and broke the silence that threatened to expose their viewing habits. "Got the keys after all. That's a relief," he said, jangling them as loudly as he could. "Let's go and find the drinking machine."

They stepped back in amongst the trees and stood together in an opening. "Everyone face in a different direction and then we won't miss it when it materialises," Phil suggested. "I'm not sure if the beam has to be aiming directly at the cruiser or if close enough is good enough. We'll have to take pot luck."

Phil held the triangular gadget about eight inches in front of him and pressed the red button. A silky voice speaking Lapertian came from the key ring - 'Thank you for purchasing a Lostall Product. Your vehicle will reappear two seconds after saying your personal password. This message was brought to you by the No Loop Holes Insurance Company. Fine print not included'.

The guys knew two hundred and seventy-seven different languages and twenty or thirty different dialects - give or take a few - from most planets in the larger star systems but, unfortunately, one of those languages wasn't Lapertian. And as they didn't understand a word the voice was saying they knew nothing about the password Phil's old man had very inconveniently forgotten to mention, so the cruiser, which was no more than twelve feet away, was stuck in a void just waiting for that all important word.

"Nothing happening over here," Tash said.

"Or here," Harri added.

"The cruiser's not appearing," Sumo said, who was by now suffering quite badly from withdrawal symptoms. "Where is the piece of shit?"

"Maybe the key ring thingy isn't working," Kam said.

"It spoke to us, or course it's working," Phil snapped.

"Yeah but it could've said anything. For all we know you might've set a self-destruct mechanism going," Marc said.

"I think my old man would've mentioned a small thing like a self-destruct mechanism so I hardly think we've blown the cruiser up. I'll try again."

Phil pressed the button twice this time. The same silky voice spoke the same foreign words, twice. Still nothing.

Phil stared at the key ring and muttered to himself. "Mmm. There has to be an easy solution. The beam is obviously not getting anywhere near the cruiser." He addressed the guys. "We'll haffta walk around until one of us bumps into something that isn't there."

The guys started moving about with their arms at full stretch feeling the air in front of them. Rather than walking forward from where they stood they were going around in circles; as if they were frightened of leaving the one spot. They were going nowhere - slowly.

Phil stopped for a moment and watched the others. "How ya gonna find the cruiser by taking little baby steps in circles? Spread out a bit more and MOVE!"

"Don't get barometric," Joc snarled.

Phil sighed. "Look, I just wanna find the cruiser, watch the discs, have a drink, relax and get away from this place, fast."

"We all do," said Marc. "None of us is having a rip-roarin' time."

"This is your fault Marc," Harri said lightly.

"Why is it my fault all of a sudden? I didn't lose the transportation."

"If you weren't getting married we wouldn't even be here," he teased.

Marc stood toe to toe with Harri. "Excuse me, but no one forced you to come. You could've stayed home and done your usual big, fat nothing with your no girlfriend and no social life. Oh sorry, I forgot, you sit and scratch your balls as you watch the home shopping show. That's always a real treat."

Harri backed away. "Drop some of the heat. I was joking." He shook his head at Marc. "I thought guys didn't lose their sense of humour until after marriage. You're way ahead of schedule. Why is it whenever anyone mentions marriage, you go all tense?"

"I don't. I just …"

"Did anyone tell you two to stop searching," Phil yelled. "I tell you, my old man's gonna get it when I get home. He should've told me how to work this stupid device. Everyone spread out a bit more."

Marc turned away from Harri, refusing to justify himself but it did get him thinking. Was he tense about getting married? He wasn't sure. Marriage didn't mean the end of your life as you knew it. Sumo was married and he still knew how to have a good time. And his folks seemed happy enough - when they were each getting their own way.

Right there was the recipe for a happy marriage - as long as someone always relented when a conflict of interest came up then everything would be fine. And, he reasoned, as long as it was always Jendee, marriage would be a piece of cake; enjoyable even. Unfortunately Marc didn't realise Jendee was thinking the same thing; that as long as HE always buckled under pressure things would go as smoothly as a day trip to Saturn on the Space Ferry Express.

The excited voice of Davis suddenly rang out into the night. "Guys, over here. I found it."

Kam's face and spirits fell. He was going home after all.

Davis was leaning at an angle of about forty-five degrees against nothing. It looked like thin air was holding him up. This was proof enough for the others that the cruiser was there. Phil aimed the key ring at a point just right of Davis's body and pushed the button. Nothing; only the dulcet tones of a voice that wasn't being as helpful as it sounded.

Phil jabbed the red button aggressively several times in succession. Still nothing except ten repeats of the message that was fast becoming extremely annoying.

They all wondered how they were gonna get home. The cruiser was there but it was of no use to anyone whilst it remained invisible.

Phil cracked. "Aaargh. That's it," he yelled at the top of his voice. "If I ever get home I swear I'm gonna make that thieving bastard sorry he pulled another shonky deal to get this useless, idiotic, pathetic…" Words failed him. He exhaled loudly and his body slumped forward. Composing himself, he looked at the guys. "At forty-six you'd think my old man would've gotten over doing juvenile…" Phil's voice trailed off as the cruiser suddenly and magically appeared before his very happy eyes. He'd inadvertently said the password.

"Yes!" Sumo jumped up and down, unable to contain his excitement. He could already taste his next drink. Life was good again.

As Phil stood there gawking at the key ring and wondering what had caused the thing to work at last, the others rushed towards the cruiser, eager to get aboard and away. In the kerfuffle, Tash trod on Phil's toes and brought him back to reality.

"Ouch. Watch where you're going, stench fiend."

"Well don't just stand there like a stunned Zibon, open the doors and let's get outta here," Tash said by way of apology.

"Did any of you bother to notice that a hubcap has been half prised off and if it's not fastened back we will lose it and then we'll have to try and replace it before I get the cruiser back to my old man?"

"E.P. will replace it," Joc said.

"No he won't. He doesn't do hubcaps or brakes. Says they're too much trouble. He only likes doing body work and anyway, these hubcaps are as rare as Spangalonian Worm shit so we'd probably never find another one."

"Just shove it back into place then," Sumo barked. "What's the big deal?"

Phil spoke through gritted teeth. "The big deal is that if I do it while the anti-theft device is still activated it'll think I'm tampering with the cruiser and render it invisible again and I'm not going through the same hassle of trying to get it back. And the other thing is - I don't know how to deactivate the device."

"Usually they're deactivated when you put the key in the door. Surely this one is no different," Sumo said through teeth that were even more gritted than Phil's. "So why don't you unlock it, let us get in, then, as an extra precaution, start 'er up, hop out and push the cap back on." His neck muscles were bulging.

Phil inserted the key into the lock carefully. The cruiser stayed put. Tentatively he turned the key. So far, so good. The red light, which was on the other side of the cruiser and whose existence was not known by the guys, went out. The anti-theft device was off. Phil reached for the door handle and pulled. The door opened easily and the cruiser sat quietly, waiting to be boarded.

"Everything seems to be in order. You guys get on and I'll fix the cap," Phil whispered. He spoke quietly because he didn't wanna risk disturbing the cruiser. Slowly he pulled the key from the lock and held onto the key ring - just in case.

The guys didn't need to be told twice. Making a mad scramble for the door and pushing and shoving each other out the way so they could get to the bar first, they got jammed in the doorway. Discs flew everywhere. They were like a bunch of wild animals fighting over the last potential mate in the universe.

"Someone's got their elbow in my temple," Joc yelled.

"Whose foot is trying to push my nuts up to my throat?" Sumo screamed.

"Looks like your own," Kam managed to say. He was squashed in the middle of the group down at about knee height.

"Hold it everybody," Marc gasped. His rib cage was being crushed and his lungs were being flattened. "Lemme squeeze through and then you can all come through one by one like civilised creatures. The drinks aren't going anywhere."

The guys stayed still as Marc wrangled his way out of the tangle of bodies. He was almost clear of the mess when Harri gave him a mighty shove in the back and sent him sprawling forward. Losing his balance he fell face first onto the floor of the cruiser. The discs dug into all the softest, fleshiest bits of his body and they hurt.

With a gap opened up the others charged in, trampling on him as they went. They had no regard for the poor buck who was merely their excuse for a depraved night out. Phil, having successfully affixed the hubcap, nonchalantly stepped over him as he entered the security of the vehicle. Marc lay there wondering why no one cared.

Sumo threw all decency aside and grabbed a full flagon of Hiten Sense, ripped the cap off with his teeth and guzzled it down without even considering using a glass. When he'd drunk half of it he pulled the neck of the bottle away from his mouth. He looked at the others. "How many drinks does that equal?" he asked.

"Half a one," Joc answered. "You haffta drink the whole flagon now to count it as one because if you lack the eloquence to use a glass then you haffta pay the price of being greedy."

"Shit. That's not fair. Who made that rule up?"

"I did."

"Since when?"

"Since I got sick of finding bits of food floating in half empty bottles of booze because someone couldn't be bothered using a glass. If you start it from the bottle, you gotta finish it from the bottle and it's only counted as one drink." Joc looked to the others. "That's fair, isn't it?"

They agreed that it was and quickly reached for glasses so they wouldn't be caught out in the same way.

"But this flagon's five litres," he whined. "Can't we make it five drinks at least?" Sumo was worried he'd never make the quota now because Hiten Sense had a bad habit of making your knees buckle and your jaw lock without any prior warning whatsoever. If that happened he'd be out of the comp.

"Sorry, them's the rules," Joc said unsympathetically.

Sumo shrugged and decided to take his chances. He put the flagon back to his lips and poured the red liquid down his throat.

"Marc, when you decide to stop feeling sorry for yourself and get up off the floor, could you close and lock the door please," Phil asked politely.

Marc looked up at the animals and snarled. They didn't notice his feeble attempt at anger; they were too busy catching up on their fluid intake. Bastards.

Struggling to his feet as noisily as he could he limped over to the door, slammed it shut and activated the fly lock. No one noticed the great effort it took for him to carry out the task. He slowly made his way over to the bar acting as if he were on death's door. No one cared. No room for sympathy around here, he realised. He quit the act and took the glass of Gernia that Kam had so thoughtfully poured for him and gulped it down thirstily.

Phil added his discs to the pile on the table, got himself four different drinks, fired the cruiser up and set the co-ordinates for home. Silently and stealthily the cruiser lifted straight up. He'd used the fly only option for this take off as there was no room for a run up. He turned all the coloured lights on, drank his drinks in quick succession and re-joined the others.

As the cruiser floated slowly towards the sky, Kam busied himself mixing various strange and exotic concoctions so everyone could get mellow again quickly and also so he wouldn't have to think too much about Sugar Anne. He looked at the Bonala Amber and the Binzi Glow but he wasn't quite ready to have them yet. He still wanted to think about her for a while longer. Then, surprisingly enough, he had what he thought was a brilliant idea. He left the confines of the bar and headed for the controls. All hope was not lost yet.

"Are we gonna watch Dolly Parton first?" Sumo asked. He'd finished the flagon and was feeling remarkably well considering how quickly he'd drunk it. Anyone else would have been clinically dead about now. He had wasted no time in getting himself another drink either. Sensibly he got it in a glass this time.

The discs lay spread out in front of them. There was so much to choose from but they all agreed on Dolly. Madonna was going on second; she was, after all, the recommended choice. But Dolly had that little bit extra to offer; and what guy in his right mind could go past that?

"Before we put a disc in let's get a really huge, potent cocktail each, kick back, relax and enjoy the show," Joc suggested.

"Well hurry up about it," Sumo said, "I'm getting antsy."

"Hey Kam, mix us something really strong and thick that'll make our minds swirl and enhance our viewing pleasure," Phil called.

No reply.

"Where is he? He's disappeared. Kam?" Phil called again.

Still no reply.

"Whatta we gonna do now?" Davis said.

Now that the guys had gotten comfy they would have sat there and slowly rotted whilst waiting for their serving boy to return but Sumo had needs, and those needs couldn't wait. He wanted to get on with the entertainment. He wanted to view the discs in this lifetime, not the next. He wanted to win the drinking competition. Nothing, but nothing, was going to stop him satisfying those needs.

He stood up. "I'll fix the drinks while Tash organises the discs. A simple solution to a simple problem." Lazy turds.

Sumo started towards the bar and saw Kam standing behind it, happily mixing away.

"Were you there all the time?"

"No. I went up front and set off a probe to find Sugar Anne and bring her to me," Kam replied casually.

"Oh. Mix us a cocktail that'll have our innards packing up and leaving for a safer place to live and come and watch the show. Before you do that, give me a glass each of Gellin, Portad, Frat and Vooma please. I'm way behind on my quota."

Kam poured the drinks. Sumo drank them. He was partially satisfied.

"What info did you give the probe about Sugar Anne? If you just described her you know it'll pick up anyone that remotely matches her description, and silicone and bleached hair ain't exactly rarities."

"I know. I had a strand of her hair so it's got her genetic info. It'll definitely only pick her up."

"And whaddya gonna do with her when you got her?" Sumo wanted to know.

"Marry her."

Sumo looked sceptical. "Yeah sure. And what if she don't wanna marry you or live on Dectarus. Then what?"

Kam shrugged. "She'll wanna marry me. She liked me. You saw how much."

"Right," Sumo answered dryly. "Drinks," he said, as he walked away.

Kam poured a bit of this, a dash of that and copious amounts of other stuff into the blender and turned it on. It whirred and clunked as it tried to cope with the amount of alcohol it was being expected to mix. It was industrial size but it had been overworked severely. It made a horrible screeching noise and stopped. At the exact same moment, all the lights went out and plunged the guys into blackness.

The cruiser was about five thousand feet above the city moving at a leisurely pace of two hundred k's. Phil had programmed it to really get moving once it hit the stratosphere.

A couple of Australian tourists, who were out searching for the alleged festive atmosphere of the city that never sleeps, happened to look up to see if they could see any stars for a change. They'd been travelling across the country for three weeks now and in all that time they'd yet to see any signs of anything twinkling.

In an unusual change of pace they noticed something much more interesting than the North Star. The rotating coloured lights that surrounded the cruiser made it a very conspicuous object in the night sky. They studied it for a moment, wondering which airline used so many lights.

"That's not a plane," Bruce suddenly realised, "that's a UFO."

"Quickly," Linda yelled excitedly as she elbowed her husband in the ribs, "get a photo. We can make a fortune."

Bruce snapped to and lifted his camera to the sky ready to capture his first UFO on film. He aimed the lens at the object, attempted to snap the picture, discovered that the high-speed, grainy, 400 ASA film hadn't been wound on from the previous shot of Linda standing in front of the Empire State Building, quickly rectified the problem, took aim again and then, without warning, the UFO suddenly disappeared. Snap, and it was gone. It didn't appear to streak away though, it just disappeared and left only the blackness of the sky.

Bruce and Linda looked at each other and then back to the sky.

"Did you get the shot?" she asked.

"I think so."

"Let's get the film developed so we can sell it before the morning broadcast." Linda knew the media would pay big for any sensationalist crap and this had 'exclusive' written all over it.

"But I've only used ten shots," Bruce whined.

"So? Soon you'll be able to buy as much film as you want."

Reluctantly Bruce agreed. They'd taken no more than half a dozen steps when something that looked like a small beam of light came rushing towards them. The light stopped in front of Linda, carried out a quick scan of her DNA, found she wasn't Sugar Anne and swirled on down the road to continue its search. The probe would not stop until it had located

Sugar and delivered her to Kam.

Linda stared open mouthed at Bruce. "Did you get a shot of that?" she asked.

Bruce shook his head.

"It doesn't matter." But it did matter because she knew the two events combined would have made for a much better, and more profitable, story. "Gimme the camera. I'll hold it in case another photo opportunity comes up. That way it won't be missed," she snarked.

Years of reading trashy rags was about to pay off. They hurried on down the street in search of their gold mine.

Chapter 16

"**K**am," Phil screamed, "what happened?"

"The blender made a funny noise then the lights went."

"Shit. We've blown a fuse. I hope we got another one." Phil felt his way to the bar, opened the cupboard that contained odds and sods for just such emergencies, found the luminosity beamer, turned it on and rifled through the container marked 'I hope what I want is here'. His old man liked to think he had a quirky sense of humour. Hope was on his side and he located a replacement fuse.

Phil hurried to the fuse unit and swapped them over. With a kind of urrgh/mmmfp sound the blender restarted and the lights came back. He looked at Kam. He had a faraway dreamy look in his eyes. Mind you, that wasn't terribly unusual, but Phil expected him to look worried, or apologetic, at least.

"Don't use the blender again, it doesn't sound too good. Just finish this drink."

Kam got eight of the biggest glasses left and filled them to the brim with his concoction. The glasses held the equivalent of fifteen double shots of scotch - if you were at home pouring your own. If you were in a bar paying a fortune for each hit, then the glasses held the equivalent of thirty double shots. Drink measures were obviously a personal thing.

Kam handed the drinks around, took a seat and waited for Tash to do his thing. Tash put Dolly in, pressed 'Action' and ran back to his chair. Music started. A twangy voice filled the room but there was no visual to go with the sound.

"Where's Dolly?" Sumo screamed after an agonisingly long minute. "Why aren't I seeing Dolly? Why isn't she sitting on my lap or pulling my hair?" One small set back and the man was on the verge of hysteria.

"Maybe it's a dud disc. I'll try a Madonna one."

"Hurry up; just hurry up." Sumo was practically wiping tears from his eyes. Sobs were not far from racking his body.

Tash replaced the disc. They waited. Some music, a voice - no visual.

"Shit," Sumo yelled, "put another one in."

The same thing happened over and over and over again. Not one of the discs Tash tried had any images that were supposed to be making their lives worth living.

Sumo was stunned. He sat there with his head in his hands, his empty glass on the floor where he'd dropped it.

"Hey, when the fuse blew would that have affected the unit?" Marc asked, really hoping it had and that it was a simple problem to fix.

"Maybe. I hadn't thought of that. There's one way to find out. Put the disc in that Rodge gave us," Phil said to Tash.

As quick as a flash the bored stripper stood before them waiting for the word.

"Well, it's not the image projection unit," Phil said. "Try a few more."

After twenty more tries they gave up. All sound, no action. Their cocktails had been drunk in a couple of anxious gulps and they'd hardly even noticed the pure germ killing power the thing contained. This was very, very bad.

They had gone to all that trouble to rip off that shop and it hadn't been worth the bother. What good was music without the suggestive movements that matched the lyric content? This, they decided, would have to go down as the most viral thing of the night.

They sat there looking very despondent wondering how they were going to end the night on a high note when all they had was one workable and semi-watchable disc.

Meanwhile, as the cruiser continued its climb towards home, the probe relentlessly pursued Sugar Anne.

In a city of millions of people, half of those millions would be female and, taking a rough guess, a good third of those would be blonde and half of those third would not be natural blondes. A further two-thirds of those non-natural blondes would not have a couple of pouches of silicone shoved inside their bodies. Of the remaining third who were bleached and surgically enhanced maybe only a sixteenth of them were exactly one hundred and seventy-two point five centimetres tall and in that group maybe only a handful of them weighed exactly sixty-four kilograms, had blue eyes and the blood type AB negative.

To further narrow the parameters of the search Kam had programmed the probe to search in a general southwesterly direction from where it was released and to cover an approximate area of forty kilometres by thirteen kilometres. He was working on the assumption that Sugar Anne would not have gone much further than those distances in the last couple of hours.

The probe, which was armed with all of Sugar Anne's vital statistics, both physical and microscopic - thanks to her strand of hair, was able to scan huge areas at a time, hone in on a possible match, do a thorough check in a few seconds and quickly determine if it had found its subject or not. So far, Sugar had eluded it.

Whizzing around the streets it was barely noticeable amongst the flashing neons. Detecting a possible match about three kilometres away it changed its course slightly and headed south, southwest. As it got nearer to its target it was detecting that this match was the closest yet.

After a hard night at work, Sugar Anne liked nothing more than to go to her favourite deli, grab an iced lemon tea and a cream cheese bagel and walk slowly home through the busy streets. Tonight she'd stopped and chatted to the McCastle's a bit longer than she normally would have. She was in a good mood for a change.

She knew her life would be changing very soon. She was close to finishing her book and she had a really good feeling about it. It just had to get published. To her, it was a lot better than half the crap that got onto the shelves. But of course she'd think that because she was the one writing it. She always took comfort in the fact that countless number of best sellers had been rejected numerous times by publishers who were too narrow sighted to know a good thing when they saw it, so she felt confident that someone, somewhere would see the value in her book. And there was no way she was going to be a stripper all her life. Good things were coming her way - she was owed them.

What she didn't know was that a probe was also coming her way; a probe that intended to take her far, far away from the city and far, far away from her life. That had definitely not been in her plans.

She said goodnight to the McCastle's and started on the walk home. She wasn't afraid to walk the streets after dark because she figured she had as much right as anybody else to be free to do what she wanted, when she wanted, as long as she never hurt anybody. She would not be intimidated by the threat of personal harm. Anyway, she was a black belt in karate so she had the edge on any would-be attackers.

The street was quiet tonight with only a sprinkling of people who were wrapped up in themselves and their own little worlds. No one noticed the light.

The probe hovered around Sugar Anne, scanning her for information.

At first she thought the light was coming from a torch or something but it was very concentrated and very bright. Before she had time to give it more thought it swiftly enveloped her and lifted her off the ground - bagel, tea and all - and began its journey back to the cruiser and the fool for love Kam.

Chapter 17

Sumo got up and made a bee-line for the bar. He'd decided that the one positive thing to come out of this screwed up night was going to be the drinking record.

"So far tonight I've drunk one hundred and three drinks," he declared. "Is that not correct?"

"That's right," Joc answered.

"Right here, right now I'm gonna drink thirteen of my choice and then you choose the last five. I'm not only gonna win, I'm gonna set a record that'll never be broken. The rest of you will never catch up unless you come and match me now - two drinks to my one. Do I have any takers?"

"I'll take the challenge," said Harri, "I'm on ninety-seven and I might as well try and hold onto the record."

Harri stood next to Sumo. Kam got them a clean glass each from which they would take all their drinks. The others were feeling a little worse for wear after Kam's last mix and they knew they'd never keep too many more down.

"I'll just check our speed and altitude and make sure we're still on schedule," Phil said. He went to the controls. Everything seemed to be in order. He looked out the window to check out the view below. One of his favourite things was to view a planet from this kind of vantage point. Usually everything looked peaceful and clean from this height. They were up at ten thousand feet now and slowly rising.

Through a gap in the clouds, the light from the torch on the Statue Of Liberty caught Phil's eye. He couldn't quite make the structure out so he was curious to see what it was that was so tall and seemingly stuck out in the middle of nowhere. Turning the white underneath light on he illuminated the statue and a large area of the surrounding water. He had to confess that it was an awesome sight.

"Hey guys," he called, "look out the windows a sec and check out the statue. It's huge."

Harri had drunk six to Sumo's three by this time and he was feeling a bit woozy. He was glad that Phil had instigated a diversion. The others were urging them on noisily and their raucous behaviour was bothering Harri's senses, which were feeling delicate.

Sumo was reluctant to leave his place at the bar but he decided that if the others were going to have a look then he would too. A short break would help push the drinks down and make room for more he reasoned, and he didn't want anything to go wrong at this stage of the game. You never knew when your guts were going to heave. It would suddenly come on without warning and Sumo had too much at stake right now to be foolish. He emptied his glass and joined the others at the windows.

The statue was an interesting sight. Of all the places they'd been they'd never seen anything to match it.

"D'ya reckon my old man could make use of that thing?" Phil asked.

"Probably. But how would he get it home?" Marc said.

"I dunno but I'm sure he'd find a way if he really wanted to. That'd look good in the middle of Wader Lake, right in front of our house, and it'd probably pull in a few tourists and quite a few zintas straight outta their pockets and into my old man's. Just think how much he could make from that thing. I'll tell him about it and see if he's interested."

"OK that was fun, now let's get back to the bar," Sumo said. He was ready for round two.

As the guys were taking their final look at the sight below an object streaked past the cruiser.

"Did you guys see that?" Davis asked. "That was no shooting star."

"Maybe another group of guys is on a buck's night and they had the same idea as us about coming here," Phil suggested.

"Can anyone see anything?" Joc asked as he craned his head from side to side trying to make out anything discernible.

"You're looking in the wrong direction guys. It's over here," Sumo said. He was looking out the opposite windows.

The guys all turned at once to see what 'it' was.

"Oh no," Davis said nervously, "it's a group of tough chicks from Amazonia."

It was indeed a group of tough chicks from Amazonia and they weren't known for their subtlety or grace.

The girls had ended up next to the guys because they'd been bored.

They were bored with going to the same old places and seeing the same old faces and they were especially bored with having to listen to Lynara going on about her string of lousy lovers - again. According to her, her latest squeeze, a tall, dark-haired hunk with the dubious name of Hardon, was good in bed. Not like the selfish prat before him - he was bloody lousy. However, that now selfish prat had been good in bed - last week, unlike the selfish prat before him - he was bloody lousy. And so it went. Every replacement was good. Every ex was lousy.

Trouble was, Lynara could never remember what she'd told anyone about anything. Facts never came into her version of events because they just got in the way of a good story and, if nothing else, she was a good storyteller. She hated when anyone questioned her; it made her huffy and if she didn't want to answer she'd just ignore the question as if it had never been asked. If Shabon and Ammily wanted the true facts about the performance quality of her many ex's they'd ask Loulla who, unbeknownst to Lynara, was equally qualified to make a judgement

To shut Lynara up for awhile, Shabon decided they needed to let their hair down and do something exciting. She'd just purchased a brand new Starbuster ZX, Model 9. It was the fully decked-out sports version with all the latest gadgets, buttons and switches complete with the extra stripes because they looked so good. The top could be removed when it was used for regular driving.

Not only was it one hot machine, the Model 9 was a very fine piece of work with the latest Energy Displacement System (EDS), affectionately called an engine. It had smooth, sleek lines and it was the leader of the next generation of vehicles that were soon to be seen in all the right places. Small and snazzy on the outside, it was huge and roomy on the inside; a standard feature on most inter-galactic vehicles. Keeping the exterior size to a minimum helped make travel over great distances easy and quick. How the inside was made bigger than the outside - no one knew. It was a closely guarded design secret that only the inventor knew how to create.

Actually, it was the great-great-great-great granddaughter of the inventor, and a few select members of her immediate family, who now held the secret. It had been passed down from generation to generation and, not for want of trying, in all that time no one else had been able to fathom how it was done and probably no one ever would. Most beings had stopped trying to figure it out a long time ago. They'd decided it wasn't worth the trouble. Rumours about it all being done with mirrors were later found to be false.

The girls got into the small, but roomy, sports machine. Shabon sat at the helm while the others made themselves comfortable in the back.

Because they weren't really dressed to go anywhere, they decided to just buzz around for awhile; put the ZX through its paces.

"If we see a nice guy," Shabon said, as she set the Starbuster in motion, "he's mine."

Ammily scoffed. "Ha! Show me a nice guy and I'll show you a woman with too much facial hair."

The ZX sped off. It raced around planets and systems as if it was an Akom stuck to the tail of a Wheezing Furbil, which, for the uninitiated, was a parasite stuck to the fastest known rodent in the entire galaxy - and then some. As nothing terribly interesting seemed to be going on in the eastern arm of the galaxy, or rather nothing they hadn't seen before, Shabon changed course and headed south. They were just having a good time being on the move.

It was as the girls did a trip around Earth they spotted the lights on the cruiser. It looked like a beacon just hanging in the air. The girls decided to investigate.

Chapter 18

The girls appeared deceptively nice.

"They're smiling and waving and holding up a comm-speak," Tash said.

"If they're smiling that could mean trouble," Davis said. "Remember last time one smiled? I got two fingers broken in an arm wrestle."

"That's 'cos you're a softie," Joc said.

"I didn't see you rising to the challenge."

"That's because I knew better than to tangle with them. Quick Phil, make contact."

Phil held up his hand to indicate to the girls he'd just be a second, ran to the controls and plugged the exterior comm-speak in. This established outside communication with anyone who had a similar system and it wasn't restricted to a one on one link. Any number of vehicles could communicate at the same time.

"OK, we're on," Phil said.

"We just came to say hi, boys," Shabon sing-songed when she heard Phil's voice. "We saw your lights on and thought we'd see who was hanging around."

"Daddy let you have the family wagon for the night, did he?" Loulla teased.

"Daddy oughta get himself something a bit nicer so you boys don't have to be seen in a stinking old rust bucket," Lynara added.

"I would be sooo embarrassed," Ammily said, with mock shame.

"If I had hair like yours, I'd be embarrassed," Phil said. "And it's pretty obvious you girlies know nothing about classic cruisers. This vehicle has got a long and illustrious history of …"

"Spare us the boring details pal," Shabon said impatiently, "we don't give a flying fig about its ancient beginnings. What we wanna know is - can it race?"

"Can it race! D'ya hear that guys? The chicks wanna know if this baby can race." The guys were looking at each other a bit worried. They didn't think the cruiser would ever be able to match the Starbuster.

Phil stayed looking at the guys so he could avoid Shabon's stare while he considered if the cruiser was up to the challenge.

"Hello, over here," Shabon clicked her fingers impatiently. "Remember us? Can the piece of broken down junk race or not? A simple yes or no will do. Come on, snap to it otherwise we'll go elsewhere for amusement."

Phil was not going to be shown up by these tough Amazonian chicks. Maybe it was time someone taught them a lesson. "Yeah, it can race," he said bravely. "You seriously wanna take us on in that inferior machine?"

"I'll show you inferior. Now, we need a set start and finish point and if you even so much as try and cheat, we'll hunt you down and when we find you - and you know we will - we'll hurt you. OK?" Shabon smiled in a way in which she thought looked sweet but it looked more like a snarl.

"OK." The guys knew she meant it.

"Choose a point and we'll get on with it," she said.

"Have we got time for this Phil?" Davis whispered nervously. "We gotta be at E.P.'s remember."

"I know, but we'll make it. I wanna race these chicks and show them a thing or two. They need humbling."

000 163 000

"Imagine living with her when her hormones go viral," Tash said. The guys shuddered.

"You're taking your time over there. Whattsa matter? Do me and my hormones scare you?"

"Wait a second, would'ya. I'm deciding where we should start and stop - unless you wanna do it?"

"We'll be here forever unless you take control," Loulla said to Shabon. "Make a decision."

"Set co-ordinates for Zero Nine C, One One S, Five Eight H. That's our start point. We'll meet you there and then decide on the rest. It's not far from here so you can take it easy if you want but don't take longer than a minute. Call it a warm up lap. We'll be waiting for you." Shabon cut communication before anyone had a chance to reply and then the Starbuster was gone.

"What about my record?" Sumo whinged.

"What about it. You can drink while I drive, can't you?"

"S'pose," he sulked. This kind of action would've been welcome about ten minutes ago but now that he'd set his mind on the record it was all he wanted to focus on.

"Sumo, you won't be affected by this. Carry on as normal and leave the hard work to me. It's not like you haffta do anything, is it?"

"Hmmph."

"Fine. Go and get another drink before you become unbearable again."

Sumo went back to his spot at the bar and resumed his task. Harri reluctantly followed.

Phil went to the controls, turned the white light off, reset the co-ordinates and made the cruiser give everything she had. They were gone in a flash and heading for the ultimate challenge.

The probe, which was thirty seconds from reaching its destination and depositing the screaming and terrified Sugar Anne in the waiting arms of Kam, was slowing down for its line up. It would attach itself to the tail end of the cruiser, lower itself into the probe bay and, when its contents were released, re-house itself in its dock. Unfortunately for it, and Sugar, the cruiser took off a tad too soon. The probe would have to continue its chase.

The cruiser scooted its way to the starting line and in forty-two seconds exactly hovered several thousand feet above an equally impressive statue at Corcovado Mountain in a place called Rio. And they had beaten the girls.

The girls pulled alongside fifteen seconds later. The guys looked at them and yawned.

"What took you girls? We were beginning to think you wouldn't show," Phil said.

"Get your hand off it pal. We decided to take our time and go via the scenic route over New Zealand, Australia and Africa," Shabon snarled.

"Big deal. Been there, done that," Joc threw in.

"Oh look, it talks. How cute," Ammily said.

"And we were beginning to think you were just a cardboard cut-out," Lynara said.

Joc scowled at them.

"Cut the chit-chat. Where are we racing to?" Phil asked.

"On our leisurely way here I thought about it and decided we should go to Saturn and do one full circuit of the outer most ring and that's it. Sound fair?"

"Too easy," Phil smirked, and hoped it would be.

"You wanna fly free or set co-ordinates?" Shabon asked.

"Fly free of course. Is there any other way to race?"

"Good. I was hoping you'd say that. To be fair we'll let the one with the eyebrows give the word. He doesn't look like he has much of a life so that little contribution to the race might give him a thrill. Ready when you are."

"We're ready. Marc, give the command when I'm at the controls. I'll tell you when."

Phil got comfortable, flicked a few switches, pushed a few buttons and laid on some extra energy. "All set," he called.

Marc looked at the girls, looked at Phil, looked at the guys, looked back at the girls and shouted, "Go." The drag was on.

The probe, which was doing its best to catch the cruiser, was again rudely left behind by a matter of seconds as Phil disappeared in a blur of coloured lights. Sugar Anne had stopped screaming because she realised it was true - in space no one can hear you scream, so instead she sat in stunned silence as they followed hot on the heels of two barely visible objects. Her spilt tea and discarded bagel remained her only links to reality.

Both the cruiser and the Starbuster took off at the exact same moment and got up to the exact same speed at the exact same time which was a surprise for the girls because they thought they'd leave the guys eating their atomic dust. Shabon put a bit more power on and got ahead of Phil. The probe raced behind.

Not to be outdone, Phil boosted the drivers. The vehicles were neck and neck. At the rate they were going they would reach Saturn in just under two minutes.

Sumo and Harri drank on, hardly noticing the phenomenal speed they were doing and hardly caring. They'd managed four and five more drinks respectively and they were feeling particularly mellow. Harri gave up on the two drinks to one business because he felt a bit off, besides which he was now only two drinks behind Sumo and he didn't want to peak too early. The others poured themselves a couple more drinks each and counted for the other two. Kam stared out the windows and watched the girls going their hardest.

Either Phil or Shabon was going to have to pull off something extraordinary because both vehicles were equal in power and resilience. What the girls didn't know was that Phil's old man had souped the cruiser up so it was one of the fastest machines in the universe. He needed the speed in case he ever had to make a quick getaway. In his line of business it paid to be prepared.

They were past the asteroid belt and heading in the general direction of Mars. Joc took Phil a drink.

"D'ya need a hand with anything?" Joc asked.

"Nah, I'm OK. Mars might be tricky though. If I can get on the inside and hug the planet, I'll be able to use the gravity to my advantage. The old man set the cruiser up so he could turn hard around planets and things and not lose any speed. Other vehicles need to go out wide and that loses time. I'm gonna pull back a bit and move over and force the girls out as wide as I can."

Phil dropped the speed off a bit. The girls thought he'd had it. They cheered Shabon on as they watched the cruiser get behind them. Phil moved over. The probe moved over. Sugar Anne stayed still.

"They're getting away," Kam called.

"Not for long," Phil called back. "I got it covered."

Mars was coming up fast. Phil put the power back on and pushed the cruiser to catch up to the Starbuster but it was having a hard time making up the ground it had lost.

"Joc, when I say so, flick that orange switch on the far corner of the panel. I gotta get alongside the girls."

"What's it gonna do?" Joc asked.

"Hopefully it'll fire up the ioniser and give us the edge we need."

"Say when."

Phil manoeuvred the cruiser a little more to the right. "Now," he yelled.

Joc flicked, the cruiser lurched, Harri collapsed into a dead faint on the floor and Davis spilt his drink - all at the same time.

The lurch was the cruiser's reaction to the ioniser. It had a bad habit of jolting the vehicle before sending it into the great, wide yonder. Harri's and Davis's little mishaps had nothing to do with anything. Davis had a clumsy attack and Harri was pissed out of his head. Sumo carried on regardless. One hundred and fourteen and counting.

Phil smirked at Shabon as he came alongside.

"How'd you get back here?" she screamed.

"That's for me to know and you to find out. This old thing ain't so broken down after all, is it girls?"

They glared at Phil. If they'd glared any harder the stress would have popped their eyes out.

Mars loomed. Phil moved closer to the girls forcing them to veer outwards. A sideswipe at these speeds would mean major bodywork repairs - and that was not on the vehicles. The girls tried to keep a tight line but Phil edged them outwards again.

Pulling hard right, Phil made a smooth turn around the planet and without missing a beat made haste for the final destination. The probe followed the same line as the cruiser.

The girls were now forced to play catch up because of the wide angle of their turn. They had to correct their course by forty degrees. The cruiser was way ahead of them by a good five seconds.

"I thought you said this thing was unbeatable," Loulla yelled to Shabon. "We're never gonna catch them now."

"Yes we will, even if you three have to get out and push." Shabon was not one for giving up easily.

"What's that?" Ammily said.

"What's what?" Loulla asked.

"That," Ammily said, pointing outside the ZX at a woman enveloped in a ball of light who was managing to keep pace with them.

Sugar Anne saw the girls looking at her. "Help," she screamed. "Help me."

Naturally they couldn't hear her. Not that they could have done anything for her anyway - it wasn't one of their probes, and they had more important things to do than rescue a woman who was better looking than they were.

Ammily shrugged at Sugar and looked away.

Jupiter was a hop, skip and jump away and Saturn would be in their sights very shortly. Phil was feeling jubilant. "When we win we'll rub their noses in it and then go straight home. That's a good end to a so-so night."

Harri, who was still a lifeless lump on the floor, suddenly lifted his head and said the four words that would send the guys into a spin. "What about the donuts?" His head collapsed back down.

"The donuts! Fuuuck, we forgot the donuts." Phil was panicked. "Shit. That means we have to go back to Earth."

"What about the race?" Joc said.

"Fuck the race. I need those donuts or I'm a dead man and you know it and we're running outta time now because we wasted so much leaving Earth in the first place."

Desperate situations require desperate measures.

Using Jupiter's gravitational pull as a sling shot, Phil catapulted the cruiser away from the direction of Saturn and back towards the Earth. The cruiser was heading straight for the girls.

The collision warning light on Shabon's instrument panel shrieked. She'd been so busy focusing on the probe she hadn't noticed Phil do his about face. As quick as a flash she veered left. The probe veered right. The cruiser cut straight through the middle of the two with a minimum of room to spare and sped off at twice the speed thanks to the extra help.

The Starbuster was out of control.

Shabon cursed as she desperately tried to regain her hold on the brand new, unmarked by shopping trolleys, Model 9. It spiralled way off course and got sucked through an atmosphere vacuum which promptly spat the ZX into the far off smelly, dirty region known as 'The Rubbish Tip' - an area of space used solely for the disposal of space junk, dust, rubbish, rotting food and old, unwanted furniture. It was the job of the atmosphere vacuums to constantly comb space and keep it clean. Normally a vehicle carrying four angry girls would not have been sucked up but as the Starbuster was spinning wildly the vacuum assumed it was discarded junk. Very rarely did anything find its way out of the Tip and very rarely did anyone visit the place. A tourist attraction it was not.

As Shabon tried to figure out how to navigate her way out of the hell hole they were lost in and get to a sector of the galaxy she knew, she could taste the moment when she would make those cheating bastards deeply sorry they had broken the rules of racing. When she, and her screaming friends, found them they were going to exact a long, painful and torturous revenge. The desire to maim the guys beyond recognition was now their only reason for living.

The probe, meanwhile, followed Phil's trail and shot itself back towards the Earth in the same way as the cruiser had. Sugar Anne decided that she was actually at home having a nightmare and so didn't let anything bother her anymore. It'll be all over soon, she thought. Just as soon as the alarm goes off.

Earth was getting awfully close, awfully fast.

"Find the co-ordinates for the donut place," Phil yelled to Joc. "They're in the log under 'donuts'."

"Can you slow this thing down, we're coming in too fast," Joc yelled back as he looked for the information.

"I'm trying but it's not responding."

"Two Eight J, Zero Two, Six Five C."

"What?" Phil seemed confused.

"They're the co-ordinates. Put them in."

Phil punched numbers and letters at the same time as trying to negotiate the re-entry. He miscalculated badly and the cruiser was heading for solid rock. If they hit, it would not tickle.

Pandemonium broke out amongst the others.

"We're gonna die, we're gonna die," Davis screamed. "I knew we shouldn't have got tangled up with those chicks."

"I don't wanna die a virgin," Tash confessed in a moment of weakness. "Somebody do something."

"Well I ain't screwing you," Marc said.

"I was on the verge of greatness," Sumo lamented. "The record was mine."

"It's nice that you think of your wife at a time like this," Kam said. He was thinking of Sugar Anne.

"Who?" Sotty was the furthest thing from his mind.

Sumo had made drink number one hundred and sixteen and the guys were just about to choose his last five when the donut thing happened. If Sumo had anything to drink from this point on that wasn't especially chosen for him, it wouldn't be counted. He didn't care anymore. He grabbed a bottle of Undone and drank for the sake of sanity. The others joined him. Marc toasted all the unborn children he'd never have. Possible death made sentimentality a compulsory thing. None of them thought about the escape pods.

"Hold on," Phil yelled. He seemed to be doing a lot of yelling. "We're coming in but I don't know how smooth it's gonna be."

The re-entry was at a shallow angle but luckily they hit water. They bounced off San Francisco Bay, like a pebble skimming off a pond, and they shot back up into the air directly under the Golden Gate Bridge. A couple of joggers saw all the action.

"They must be making another Star Trek movie," one of them said disinterestedly as they plodded on by without giving the scene a second thought. They didn't even notice the probe doing the same thing.

Touching the water had slowed the cruiser down to a manageable speed. Correcting itself with little effort, it raced on towards the set destination.

Phil sat back. All the blood had drained from his face and he was shaking. "I need a drink." He stood up and let the cruiser go on her merry way.

Sugar Anne knew this was no dream when she hit the water because it hurt. She knew now she'd been abducted by aliens, but this was not the way it was supposed to be. You were supposed to be unconscious. You were supposed not to remember; have only vague flashbacks and wonder why your life was slowly falling apart for no apparent reason. This sucked big time and she intended to tell her kidnappers just that. She was angry now and someone was gonna get it - both barrels. She'd handled gropers at the club and loonies on the streets so she was damn sure she could handle a couple of aliens.

Phil grabbed the remains of the bottle of Undone out of Sumo's hands and drank it down without pausing for a breath. He hoped there was no damage to the cruiser that couldn't be fixed. The cruiser had come to a full stop because it was at its destination but Phil didn't care. "Get me another," he asked anyone. "Make it strong."

Finally the probe caught the cruiser, attached itself and sank slowly into its bay. Sugar Anne was glad to be still. Considering the speed and distance she'd travelled she felt physically fine, except for the slight stinging in her butt cheeks. The probe had created a perfect environment for her and kept it constant. This little episode was going in her book. Where she was gonna fit it she didn't know, but she'd find a spot for it even if she had to rewrite the whole bloody thing.

Phil drank the drink that Kam proffered. He felt better. "Marc, go and get the donuts," he said without looking at him, "and make it snappy. We haven't got much time."

"Why me?"

"Because you're the buck and because I said so. You've gotten off lightly tonight. You should be thankful. If you do this we won't tie you to the back of the cruiser and tow you home naked. We haven't got time for anything now. Go. You got one minute."

"Open the door then."

Phil returned to the controls. He opened the door and walked back to the guys. "Who sent out a probe?"

"I did," Kam said.

"Why?"

"To get Sugar Anne for me."

"Well she's in the bay. Go and get her."

Chapter 19

While Marc lowered the steps and raced down to get the donuts, Kam and the others, minus Harri who was still out cold, made their way to the back of the cruiser. Phil opened the probe bay. Sugar Anne saw them and she did not look pleased and they didn't look like aliens. Aliens were supposed to have funny shaped heads with big eyes. What was going on?

Kam boldly walked to the pod, switched it off and Sugar Anne was released from its cocoon. She stood up and gave Kam an upper cut to the jaw. He sprawled backwards.

"Who the fuck do you think you are?" she raged at him. She looked at the guys looking at her. Recognition dawned. "I know you. You're the guys who were thrown out of the club. Let me tell you, I know karate so don't even think about trying anything." She assumed a threatening stance.

They remained unmoved. This was Kam's show.

Kam staggered to his feet. She punched him again because he was there. "And what's with the flying all over the galaxy crap? Did you think I might need some excitement in my life?"

"We didn't know you were ..." Phil started.

"... Whose stupid idea was it? Huh? Huh?"

Kam crawled a suitable distance away and picked himself up again. "It was mine," he said feebly. "I love you and want to marry you."

"You what!"

"I thought you'd want to because of the way you were in the club."

Oh my God. Unbelievable. This guy would be the type who'd call a phone sex hotline and believe he was talking to a living Barbie doll who wanted him desperately because she was just soooo hot for him, baby. Sugar should have felt sorry for the deluded fool, but she didn't.

"Listen buddy, I do that same routine twice a night, six days a week. You're not the first and you won't be the last. I'm a serious writer, thank you very much, and I do what I have to until the day arrives when I don't have to put up with crap from guys like you who seem to think I need rescuing, or whatever shit it is you think I need. I wouldn't marry you if you were the last man, alien, whatever, left in the whole goddamn universe."

Kam looked hurt, really hurt. Never had he felt so dejected. His stature went from erect to hunched over. He slunk towards her.

"Furthermore," she said as she poked her finger at him, "you ruined my dinner and I got iced tea all over me. Look at this, it'll never come out. Are you going to pay my dry cleaning bill? I oughta sue you for … for…" She couldn't think what for. Pity she wasn't Nampereon. She'd have owned half the galaxy by now.

Blah, blah, blah. On and on she went. "I am sick and tired of people assuming they can have a piece of me any time they damn well feel like it. You have no idea how... what are you doing? Keep away from me you …"

Kam pressed the pod and the probe enveloped her again with its light. She was still ranting but her voice was going nowhere. He told the probe to take her back to the point where it had picked her up and set her free. She was a wild woman. He had been deceived - big time.

The probe obeyed and Sugar Anne disappeared into the night.

"What's her problem?" Joc was surprised by her attitude.

"Too wild for you Kam," Tash said.

"I warned you all," said Davis. "It's the pollution that makes them that way."

"Women! Can't do anything right by them," Phil said, shaking his head. "Anyway, time's up. We gotta scoot."

They walked back to the main body of the cruiser. The door was still open and Marc wasn't back. Harri had rolled over onto his side and was sucking his thumb. He was also hugging his beat up shoe as if it were a teddy bear. At least he was asleep now which meant he'd regained consciousness at some point in the last minute.

"Where's Marc with those donuts?" Phil said impatiently.

Marc scrambled up the steps at top speed. "Quick, lock the door and get outta here," he panted. "Move it, unless you want trouble."

In his haste to get the donuts and be back aboard the cruiser in one minute, Marc had made a big mistake.

The cruiser was back in New York, but not the city. It hovered quietly above a donut shop that was located upstate, on the NYC Throughway.

Having no money to purchase the donuts didn't bother Marc; they'd gotten by all night without any. What did worry him was that he was the one risking his neck for Phil, just because he was the buck. What a lousy rule that was. When he got home he was going to find the book on buck's night etiquette and check to see if doing all the dirty work was part of his obligations. He felt sure that it wasn't.

Once on the ground Marc ran towards the building. He flung open the doors, raced to the counter, spotted a box of donuts, picked them up, counted them and found only five. He needed six. He looked at the counter clerk who was about to take a bite from the missing donut, lunged forward and ripped it out of his hands. Thankfully it was still in one piece.

Marc shoved it in the box, closed the lid, and ran out of the building without so much as a thank you.

It was while he was heading back towards the cruiser that he realised his mistake. There were two separate buildings side by side. The building next to the one he'd just left was advertising donuts. The building he'd just robbed was advertising Police.

Marc's heart leapt into his mouth. It was official - he was a low-life criminal. Fancy stealing from the cops. What had he been reduced to? He ran on, too scared to look back to see if anyone was following him.

Sergeant O'Malley left the donuts with Sergeant Tyler and went to get them both a cup of coffee. Night duty was long and boring out here on the Throughway. Tyler shuffled piles of paperwork from one side of the desk to the other. He liked to see which side of the desk they looked better on. He didn't actually have any intention of doing any of it. The day shift boys and girls could take care of it.

He opened the donuts and looked at the selection. Sprinkles or no sprinkles, that was the question. What went best with coffee - the pink icing or the yellow? Decisions, decisions. What did his taste buds say? He smacked his lips together a few times to help him decide. Sprinkles - blue ones.

The donut was centimetres from his salivating mouth when the box was rudely snatched away by some desperado who had rushed in from who knew where. He'd seen some bad clothes before, but this guy was way out there. Tyler sat there stunned. This guy had a wild look; he was high on something. Before he could blink, his carefully chosen donut was cruelly taken from him. Then the guy was gone. That was it. All he'd wanted was the donuts. Shit, they had a whole shop full of 'em next door, why couldn't he have gone there? Now he'd have to get up and walk next door to replace them. O'Malley would be as mad as hell.

O'Malley brought the coffees in.

"Where's the donuts?" he asked, eyeing Tyler suspiciously. "Did you eat the whole lot? I'm good enough to go an' get 'em, an' make you a coffee, an' what thanks do I get - you go an' stuff the whole lot down your throat without any thought for me. Who are you … Homer Simpson? I'll remember this."

Tyler was sure he would. O'Malley was very good at guilt. Said he got it from his mother.

Tyler couldn't be bothered trying to explain what had happened. O'Malley wouldn't believe him anyway. He preferred to think the worst.

"Yeah I ate 'em. Sorry, I got carried away. I'll get some more."

Tyler neatened his pile of paperwork, left his desk and went next door to replace the pilfered goods.

O'Malley watched him go and wondered how Tyler had the cheek to get offended anytime someone made a joke about cops and donuts when Tyler himself was a living, breathing example of the cliché. Goddamn hypocrite.

Chapter 20

Phil locked the door and hot-footed the cruiser out of there as fast as he could. They were gone before Tyler even made it to the door. They were heading home at last.

Marc put the box of donuts on the bar. "Kam, fix me a Yellow Belly."

Yellow Belly's were an especially good drink when you were feeling nervous or scared. They were Davis's favourite drink.

Kam served it to him in a carafe and put a straw in it so Marc wouldn't drink it too quickly. A drink time of five minutes or more was highly recommended because of its powerful effects. If it was drunk too quickly Marc might find himself attempting to leap from the cruiser into space because of the sudden feeling of bravery it gave you. Marc knew the risks and drank slowly. He decided to let the drink see him home.

Phil could relax now that he had everything under control. "Ever notice how much crap Earthlings shoot up here?" he asked as he joined the conscious ones for a drink. "I'm gonna call Hover Suck next week and get them to send an atmosphere vac 'round here. It could do with a bloody good clean up. So far this trip, according to the nav read-out, we've dodged communication satellites, spy satellites, weather satellites, general space junk like old rockets and stuff and just then we had a near miss with a huge telescope. It's getting so it's dangerous to fly. At least we know the scanners and avoidance systems work. The old man was beginning to wonder about that."

"Pity the avoidance system can't dodge outta control rocks. S'pose there's not much you can do about those things," Marc said.

"Talking about outta control, can we quickly finish this competition now?" Sumo asked.

"OK, it's pretty obvious none of us are gonna catch you now and your nearest rival is drooling on his shoe, so we need to take a vote on the five worst drinks of the night," Joc said.

"Tequila," Tash said.

They all agreed on that.

"That foul smelling one that comes from Hereton," Phil said. "What's it called?"

"Dump Juice," Kam said.

"That's the one. All agree? Yep. OK."

"Cat Piss," Davis offered.

"Which one was Cat Piss?" Joc asked.

"It's not actually called Cat Piss, it just tastes like it. It's that cheap white wine that could dissolve enamel."

"That's a definite yes," Phil said.

"Two more. How about Rend Numb. That was off," Marc said.

"Literally, I think," Joc said. "I don't ever remember it tasting that bad but if we all agree, he has to drink it."

They all agreed.

"For the last one I say he waits 'til we get to E.P.'s and has that disgusting, thick, slimy stuff that E.P. keeps on the top shelf. It's like drinking a cup of phlegm. If that doesn't end his chances for the record, nothing will," Phil said.

Yeah, they liked that idea.

Sumo felt ill at the thought of what lay ahead. He wished he hadn't put so much emphasis on breaking the record now. But it was too late, he was committed.

The cruiser was making good time on its trip home. The guys would make it to E.P.'s with maybe a minute to spare. He'd need the cruiser for about an hour and then Phil could deliver it home without so much as a scratch and his old man would let him use it again if he needed to. It was a good thing Joc thought ahead.

As Kam was organising Sumo's final drinks, a banging sound came from the rear of the cruiser.

"Did you guys hear that?" Phil asked.

"Was it the probe docking?" Kam suggested.

"Nah, that was back just after Marc got the donuts. Sugar Anne sure had one quick trip back to wherever."

Kam felt a little pang when her name was mentioned. She may have abused him but he couldn't help but feel something for her still. Now was the time to forget, he decided. Bravely he poured a Bonala Amber with a Binzi Glow. He'd sip it slowly so her memory would fade slowly.

"If you're worried, check it out," Joc said.

"Think I might, just in case." Phil left the group and went to investigate the noise. "Hey guys," he called. "Come here. D'ya reckon my old man would want this?"

Stuck to the tow bar of the cruiser was a large object with the word 'Voyager' stencilled to its body.

In a purely random act of chance that not even the world's biggest computer could have calculated the odds of happening, 'Voyager', travelling in an east/west line to the cruiser's north/south, struck the rear of the cruiser and got a section of itself tangled up. The object had been sent by Earthlings into outer space in the hope it would be found by extraterrestrial life. The further hope was that, upon finding the expensive gift containing messages, books, music and the like, it would ensure friendly and non-hostile contact with Earth's outer worldly neighbours. The trouble was

- no such neighbours had ever bothered to pick it up when they'd come across it because everyone assumed it to be a piece of debris the vacuum was yet to catch up with. Until now it had gone unwanted and ignored.

"What is it?" Tash asked.

"I dunno, but my old man might be able to find a use for it. There's no way I'll be able to shake it off. If it falls away before we get home, then it does. If not, my old man gets a pressie."

"Leave it then. It's not hurting anything," Marc said. "Now let's see if Sumo has got what it takes."

Kam handed Sumo the bottle of Tequila. He had to drink the remaining contents of the chosen bottles. Sometimes you got lucky and only had a mouthful to contend with. The Tequila was a third full, complete with worm.

"What's that floating in the bottom of the bottle?" Sumo wanted to know before he put the bottle to his lips. "It looks suspiciously like a Jubantan Slug Creature. If it is, I don't haffta drink it. Nowhere do the rules say you haffta eat poisonous things."

"It's part of the drink. It won't kill you. Just let it slide down your throat, nice and easy," Joc said.

"You sure you wanna do this 'cos if you can't handle it, we'll understand." Tash gave Sumo a chance to back out.

"I'll do it." He closed his eyes, brought the bottle to his lips and tipped his head back. The guys cheered as the bottle drained and the worm disappeared. Marc felt sick just watching it.

"Next," Sumo spluttered.

Kam gave him the Dump Juice. You really needed a peg on your nose for this one but Sumo had the advantage of not being able to smell it anyway. The bottle was half full. Sumo groaned when he saw how much he had to down. He took a deep breath, closed his eyes again and gulped down whilst breathing out through his nose, which was no mean feat.

"Finished." He gasped for air. He was nearly half way there but he was feeling incredibly sick. "Next."

Kam handed him the Cat Piss. This one was only a quarter full. Sumo was visibly relieved. Eyes closed, head back, mucous membranes stripped and he was done.

As Kam was handing Sumo the Rend Numb his stomach started convulsing.

"Hold on," he said. He had gone a sickly yellow colour. He turned towards the toilet and was deciding if he needed to puke but nothing was happening other than the flip-flops. A small burp escaped his lips, and that was it. He turned back, his colour was coming good and he took the drink from Kam. The bottle was half full. He was doing it hard, no doubt about it.

"That was close," he said. "I thought for sure I was gonna lose the lot." With renewed vigour he downed the second to last drink. His tongue lost all feeling and his arms went tingly but nothing could dampen his enthusiasm. "Only one off. Victory is mine. How long 'til we get to E.P.'s?"

"Should be just about there," Phil said. And he was spot on. The cruiser made a smooth landing at the Stardust with not a second to spare. Voyager's landing wasn't so smooth. It bounced up and down a bit but it looked undamaged.

E.P. was patiently waiting.

Chapter 21

"Right on time boys. That's what I like to see. Had yourselves a good night then? What's that?" E.P. asked, pointing at Voyager.

"Dunno. It attached itself on the way home. I'm gonna give it to my old man. He'll love it. Just work around it, it shouldn't get in the way. There's a load of Zippy Mowers that need fixing too. We'll be in the bar. If Harri wakes up, send him in. Thanks."

"You got my fee?"

"I nearly forgot. Marc, get the donuts."

Payment for panel work was a six-pack of donuts and that was all. E.P. didn't travel anymore and the only place you could get the things was from Earth. More visits had been made to Earth for donuts alone. E.P. made his money from the bar and occasionally singing at birthday parties.

"Sumo, you got two minutes left to complete your task," Joc said as they walked into the bar. "How you feeling?"

"Not bad. I can do it."

"And Marc, you got two minutes left in which to throw up one more time otherwise you're gonna get the Buck's Special. How you feeling?"

Marc had forgotten all about that. There was no way he was gonna be able to chuck now. He wasn't drunk enough anymore and if you were caught trying to make yourself vomit the penalty was worse. He'd tried to think of how he could do it. Nothing came to mind short of sucking warm sick through a smelly sock and he didn't think that was available from the bar.

"Kenny, you old dirt bag. How you goin'," Phil said to the barman. "Busy night?"

"Yeah. We had a group of wowsers in here but E.P. sorted them out. Normally he don't like hurting women but these girls were wildcats."

"They weren't Amazonian were they?" Davis asked.

"No. Locals."

"Phew." Davis was afraid the girls had found out where they were from and had come to hurt them, as promised. He had the feeling he'd be looking over his shoulder for the rest of his life.

"Where's Harri?" Kenny asked. He was conspicuous by his absence.

"Collapsed on the cruiser. He couldn't handle the pace. He and his shoe are getting intimately acquainted, even as we speak."

Kenny didn't ask for elaboration because he didn't wanna know. Some stuff was just too weird for him.

"Could you get Sumo that bottle of thick, slimy stuff up there please," Phil said, pointing to the top shelf.

Kenny got it down and placed it in front of Sumo. "You want a glass?"

"Na. He'll drink it straight from the bottle. Put it on my old man's bill."

Sumo looked at the yellow gunk. He turned the bottle around to see what it was called. 'Monkey Vomit'. Even the name was disgusting. Sumo sighed.

"One minute left. Start drinking," Marc said. He hoped that watching Sumo trying to get it down his throat would make him heave.

"It's only a third of a bottle. It's not that hard," Joc urged.

Sumo closed his eyes and tried to think of his warm bed. He managed a couple of mouthfuls before he took the bottle away. Swallowing was hard because his stomach was making his throat close up in the hope he'd give up and have a glass of water instead.

"Only a few more mouthfuls. You can do it," Tash said as he sipped a delicious Blossom Nectar.

Sumo wondered why he put himself through this kind of shit.

"Twenty seconds. You've come this far, finish it," Davis said. He too had a delicious drink.

Sumo figured there were four more mouthfuls. The bottle went back to his lips. One gulp, one swallow. One gulp, one swallow. One …

Suddenly a banshee like scream filled the bar area.

"Reginald," Sotty shrieked, using Sumo's real name.

Sumo leapt about ten feet in the air and dropped the bottle. The mouthful of drink went down with a huge gulp of air. His stomach recoiled in horror.

Sotty stood in the doorway of the bar. Sumo didn't even turn around to acknowledge her. He was looking at the floor where the bottle lay. Not a drop of the gooey liquid had been spilt. One more mouthful remained. He had ten seconds left. All he had to do was reach down, retrieve it and be done with it. Sotty was not going to take away his moment of glory.

He leant over and grappled for the bottle. His hand made contact and he quickly put it to his lips. In a show of strength and determination he sucked the last of the liquid out of the bottle and into his mouth. All he had to do now was swallow but the air bubble felt like it was blocking off his oesophagus.

"Three, two, one, bzzz. Time's up," the guys shouted in unison.

Sumo turned to the guys and opened his mouth wide to show them that the drink was gone. He smiled the biggest smile any of them had ever seen. It truly was a proud moment. His stomach, however, did not think so and he still had to keep it down for five minutes to be the true champion and he was feeling really ill.

Sotty marched up to the bar and, in a rare and unusual display of affection, put her arms around Sumo. This was the last thing Sumo had expected.

"I missed you schnooky," she said through pouty lips. "I thought you said you'd be home hours ago and I was getting so lonely." She gave his ear a quick nibble. "When I saw you sitting here drinking I thought you were trying to avoid me."

He was, but she didn't need to know that.

"Are you coming home now? You must be so tired after your big night out." Sotty was smoothing Sumo's hair. This woman really ran hot and cold in the old mood stakes.

Sumo couldn't move or speak. He knew his victory was gonna be very short lived if Sotty didn't stop with the sickly sweet shit. Five minutes. If she would only be quiet for five minutes. His stomach was churning more violently with every word she spoke. He realised he preferred her when she wasn't being so nice. He was used to that.

Joc could see that Sotty was upsetting Sumo's delicate disposition. As a true friend he should really take advantage of it. Sumo was sweating, his colour had a greeny tinge and he was staring straight ahead, not blinking.

"Sumo, are you all right?" Joc asked politely. "You look a little off."

He didn't respond.

"Sotty, I think you should take Sumo home, tuck him into bed and smother him in kisses. He's had a tough night and all he needs now is some of your tender loving care. A bowl of your fabulous boiled sausages in white water ... er, sauce, would top it all off nicely."

Sotty was infamous for her ability to take perfectly good food and turn it into a pile of inedible, unappetising crap.

As an after thought Joc added, "Maybe even sing him a song as he goes off to sleep. That would be nice, wouldn't it Sumo?"

Sumo twitched and his stomach rolled but he continued to stare.

Something was keeping him mesmerised. Joc looked to where Sumo's eyes were fixed. Of course! He was staring at the clock, counting down five minutes. He had a little under three to go.

For Sumo, time was dragging mercilessly. He was in agony. He wished everyone would stop talking or just go away. Joc was being a bastard with his 'do this, do that' crap, making him feel sicker. Sotty kept touching his hair and face. It was driving him to distraction, but he dared not move or speak because he knew he would be throwing up a whole night's worth of booze for at least the next four hours if he did. All he wanted to do was curl up somewhere quiet and go to sleep. A long, deep, peaceful sleep.

Marc was so busy focusing on Sumo and his situation he'd completely forgotten his 'last chance chuck' had expired. The others hadn't. Turning their attention away from Sumo, who was not doing anything more interesting than changing an assortment of colours, Joc decided to bring the subject up.

"So guys, what's the Buck's Special gonna be tonight?"

They scratched their chins and pretended to be giving the question some serious thought.

"Should it involve nakedness?" Phil asked.

"Nah. Too obvious," Davis said.

"Should it involve threat to life and limb then?" Phil asked again.

"The Portable Torture fell into that category," Davis said.

"True. How about putting him on the next slow moving barge outta here and telling Jendee he's done a runner," Joc suggested.

"Not bad, but the next barge won't be leaving for another two days," Tash said.

"That's bad luck. He should really get a double whammy 'cos he had a shower. Any ideas Kam?" Joc asked.

Kam, whose memory was now free of Sugar Anne and her scornful words, tried to think of how best to get Marc. He already had eyebrows so doing something else to his body would be neither here nor there. He couldn't think of anything. By nature, he wasn't cruel. He shook his head, "Sorry, nothing comes to mind."

If Marc could've, he would have left right then and there but being the buck he had to stay 'til the last. He felt like breaking with tradition and making his escape. What could they do to him, he wondered, that was worse than what they probably already had in mind? He wished they'd just get on with whatever it was so he could go home.

"I've got it! Joc said. "Back in a sec." He walked out of the bar.

Sumo had been listening to the guys deciding on Marc's fate. Poor bastard, he thought. The clock told him he only had a minute to go but he felt his resolve fading with each second that passed. He thought the win was going to be a piece of cake and that he'd be smashing the record to bits by now. The thought of alcohol was making his mouth salivate excessively, like it does just before you vomit.

Sumo swallowed hard several times. He made a vow right then that he would never, ever drink like this again. It wasn't worth it. In fact, he was going to give up alcohol completely. He may have said the same thing a few times in the past, but this time he meant it.

Joc came back into the bar just as Sumo's final minute finished its laboriously slow way around the clock face. Sumo couldn't yell or jump for joy. His victory couldn't be enjoyed.

"Sumo, you champion," Tash yelled. "I don't believe you actually did it. Kenny, pour us all a drink. Sotty, you want one?"

"No thanks. And neither does Sumo."

If Sumo could have thanked her, he would have. Another drink was definitely the last thing he wanted.

"Of course he wants another one," Phil said. "The party's not over yet."

It was for Sumo. His body slumped forward and his forehead hit the bar. He was history.

"Bring him home when you're done please," Sotty said. "I can't be bothered hanging around. Good luck Marc. I hope they go easy on you - for Jendee's sake." Dickheads, she thought, as she walked away.

Kenny poured drinks for them.

"To Sumo," Joc toasted. "Long may he reign as the king of the mighty beverage."

They clinked glasses and drank.

"He is still alive, isn't he?" Davis asked.

Joc poked him. "Don't sweat it. He's still soft and warm. He'll be OK tomorrow. I hope."

"We got a body count of two. Not bad for a night's work," Phil said. "Are we gonna make it three?" He poked Marc in the ribs.

"Doncha think you put me through enough already? You can take a tradition too far, you know."

"We know, but we don't care. The fun goes on 'til the cruiser is fixed, then we'll leave you in peace. You're only snarky 'cos it's you who's gonna get it. You wouldn't care if it was one of us in your place. Sumo would vouch for that, if he was conscious," Joc lectured.

Joc called Kenny over, whispered conspiratorially and slipped something into his hand. Kenny nodded.

Marc watched Kenny closely. "What did you tell him?" he asked, feeling rightly paranoid.

"To fix you a Weekend Waster."

"And you had to whisper that? What's the big secret?"

"Nothing," Joc replied vaguely.

"I don't trust you. What if I refuse to drink it?"

"You can't, you're the buck," Phil said. "We'll pour it down your throat if we have to."

"Loosen up, you're supposed to be having a good time," Tash said. "Go with the flow. Enjoy yourself."

Maybe Tash was right. He'd gotten all tense and it was his big night out. He shouldn't even care about what was in store. He knew they wouldn't kill him, so what could be worse than that?

Kenny put the drink in front of Marc. He looked at it closely. There didn't seem to be anything unusual about it. It was the same colour as always and it smelt the same. He took a sip. It tasted the same. In fact, it tasted really good. Marc hadn't had a Weekend Waster in a long time. Maybe he should get back into the swing of things; it wasn't so bad. The guys were having fun and so should he.

Marc drank the drink quickly, put the empty glass on the bar and asked Kenny for a Great Time.

Joc walked towards Marc, swivelled his bar stool around and, before Marc could react to what was going on, Joc fused the zip of the protection suit closed with the mini laserweld he'd borrowed from E.P. Marc was sealed inside the suit.

The protection suit was made from a special mix of fibres that couldn't be cut, torn, burnt, melted, dissolved or clawed frantically from the body. The only way in or out was via the zip.

Marc looked horrified. "You rotten bastard. How am I supposed to get this off?"

"That's the least of your worries. We popped a laxative in your drink. In twenty-two minutes precisely you're gonna really panic. If you hadn't had a shower and changed your clothes, you wouldn't be in this predicament. Told you there was a penalty for cleanliness."

Marc went white. "Fuck you! You are a supercilious, smarmy, obnoxious, idiotic ..." His anger had cut his thinking off and he suddenly needed a leak. Why did that always happen? Your brain was never on your side.

Your brain suddenly gets informed that you cannot go to the toilet and so it tells your bladder it's full and should be immediately emptied. Stupid, useless, good for nothing brain. Then your brain knows you are calling it everything under the sun so it decides that the capacity of your bladder is significantly less than it used to be and the urge gets out of hand.

So you beg your bladder not to explode and tell your brain you're sorry for abusing it but it's too late. Your brain does not accept feeble apologies because it knows you don't really mean it. Consequently, you're stuffed.

"Reverse the fusion and get me out of this thing," Marc yelled.

"If you get hyped up, the laxative works quicker," Joc calmly informed him.

And so ended Marc's thoughts of rejoining the fun. He was in big trouble. He hated Joc. Absolutely hated him. He hoped he would be laughing about this in years to come but he doubted it very much. Some of the protection suits had facilities for going to the toilet, but this one didn't.

The one Marc was wearing was used more for protection against harsh weather and nasty bugs. The boots weren't detachable. The other type of suit, which was used for exploration into unknown areas or a good disguise if you were doing something you shouldn't, came complete with a helmet that covered the entire face. Special breathing apparatus was built in and the eyes were cameras. The shape of the eyes were large and elongated which allowed for a wide view of two hundred and seventy degrees. The boots, like the ones on Marc's suit, weren't detachable either.

Marc hadn't wanted much for his night out - just a lot of drinks and a lot of naked women surrounding him. Instead he got brutalised, tortured, abused and trapped in a suit with the threat of his bowels giving way in a flurry of unwanted activity.

"How about the mercy rule?" he suddenly said.

"What mercy rule?" Joc asked.

"I dunno exactly, but I'm sure there is one."

"No mercy rule as far as I'm aware. You guys know anything about it?"

Nah. No one knew.

"Actually, yes there is," Kam said.

Marc's eyes lit up.

"Oh no. I was thinking of the three chucks rule. Sorry Marc."

"You guys have got no idea about fair play. Doncha think this is going just a little too far?"

Nah. They didn't think so.

Davis sniffed the air. "Tash, you stink."

"What. I didn't do anything."

"Well where's that smell coming from?"

"You haven't shit your pants already have you Marc?"

"Na. I thought it was Tash too."

Joc walked over to Sumo and sniffed, which was a really silly thing to do. He recoiled in horror. "Whoa. He stinks like nothin' I ever smelt. Come up close you guys and get a lung full of this."

"No thanks, we're not that stupid," Tash said.

"It's time to get the drunk trolley I think," Joc said. "Kenny will you do the honours."

Sumo was sweating profusely as his alcohol filled body tried to get rid of some of the toxins. The odour was a result of all the drinks combined and it was an acrid, repugnant smell. Combined with Sumo's normal off-ness it made for a very dangerous aroma. The guys suspected it could be highly toxic and hoped Sumo wouldn't spontaneously combust in the bar area.

Kenny wheeled the drunk trolley to Joc. "You'll have to put him on yourself. I'm not going near him."

The drunk trolley was a simple sack trolley. The guys would have to get Sumo off the stool and prop him upright on the trolley so they could wheel him outside, but no one wanted to touch him.

"Pass us four of your big towels would you Kenny," Joc asked.

Kenny handed them to Kam.

"OK, what we're gonna haffta do is put a towel around his neck and feet and two around his middle."

Phil went to swivel the bar stool around.

"Don't do that yet," Joc yelled. "The bar being in the way of his head is the only thing holding him upright. Kam you take his feet. Put the towel under his ankles and grab the ends in one hand each. Phil and Tash you put your towel under his hips and take a side each. Davis and Marc, you do his chest. I'll take his neck. Let's do this quickly and cleanly. When we're ready I'll nod my head so we all move at the same time, and make sure you got a tight hold."

The guys took a deep breath each and got into position around Sumo. The maximum amount of time they'd be able to hold their breath would be about one and a half minutes because they had to physically exert themselves as well. Even though they weren't breathing in, Sumo's odour was still sneaking up their noses ready to singe their nose hairs. Joc gave the nod.

With a mighty heave the guys dragged and pushed Sumo sideways off the stool. The sudden thud of his full weight falling into the towels caught the guys off guard. They hadn't expected him to be so heavy. He tipped sideways towards Davis and Tash. Thinking he was going to crash land onto the floor and take him down with him, Davis gasped.

The stench that filled Davis's nose and mouth was like nothing he had ever known. Instinctively he brought his hands to his face to block off his olfactories. As soon as he let go he realised what a stupid thing he'd done. He had upset the delicate balance.

Grappling for his end of the towel, which was hanging loosely in Phil's hands, he tried vainly to correct the situation, but it was too late. The guys needed to breathe and they couldn't hold on. Sumo finished the roll he started and unceremoniously landed with a crash on the floor collecting Davis and Tash on the way down. Sumo lay across their torsos, crushing them half to death.

The guys looked horrified but Sumo didn't even flinch. He was still out cold. Neither of them could pull their bodies out from underneath.

"Get him off," Tash managed to gasp in broken spurts as he tried to roll Sumo away. Davis was a bright red colour and he couldn't even talk.

The guys couldn't help themselves. They knew the situation was potentially serious but it was funny. So funny, in fact, they laughed so hard they thought they would die.

"You fuckin…" Tash managed before being overwhelmed by the smell. He shut up quickly to try and cut down on his inhalation rate.

"Quickly guys," Joc said, tears streaming down his face, "we gotta get him off."

Marc suddenly stopped laughing and doubled over in agony. His cruel laughs at the misfortune of Davis and Tash had made his abdominal muscles massage his intestines, thus moving things along a bit. The laxative was letting him know that it would be exiting his body fairly soon and would he please find a toilet so the event could be over with promptly.

The cramp in his intestines was horrendous. He couldn't keep himself upright anymore. He dropped to the floor, lay on his side and hugged his knees to his chest to try and stop the pain. He was sweating as much as Sumo. At least the urge for a leak had left him. Without warning he let out a huge fart that seemed to last a full minute.

"Marc's shit himself," Phil shouted delightedly. He was helping roll Sumo away from the flattened and frantic bodies of his mates.

Marc finished expelling the wind and lay still. The cramps had subsided. He felt better. Tash and Davis were free of Sumo and gasping for fresh air outside the bar.

Marc stretched his legs out to test if he could stand up. He seemed OK. "Sorry to disappoint you, but I haven't shit myself yet," he said as he made his way up slowly.

"You sure? It bloody sounded like it," Davis said. He seemed a little disappointed.

"Give it time," Joc said. "Give it time."

Sumo lay peacefully on the floor, blissfully unaware of anything.

"We gotta move him outside," Phil said. "His stench is getting worse."

"We'll haffta roll him out. Getting him on the trolley now is gonna be impossible," Joc said. "Tash, Davis, get in here."

Reluctantly the guys came back inside. They headed straight for the bar and got a drink.

"Forget the drinks," Joc said. "We gotta get Sumo outta here. We'll just push him with our feet."

The guys lined up along the length of Sumo's body.

"If we push at the same time, he'll roll out easily," Joc said. "And don't stuff it up this time Davis."

Moving Sumo's body was like trying to roll a beached whale back into the ocean. He wasn't fat but he was a large, stocky build. The six of them could barely manage it but slowly they made their way towards the doors. It was thirsty work.

Halfway there, Marc's guts cramped up again. "Let me out of the suit," he begged Joc. "I'm not gonna be able to hold on much longer." He was gasping as he spoke and clutching his abdomen. He couldn't help them roll Sumo anymore.

"I tell you what. When Sumo is safely in the parking lot and I've had a drink for all my troubles, I'll think about it."

Chapter 22

Marc wanted to know how Joc got away with being an absolute bastard. He never seemed to be on the receiving end of anything. That was probably because he was usually the one instigating the trouble and strife.

But Joc would never get it. He was one of the lucky ones. There are some who give and some who receive and Joc was a giver and it took a lot to faze him. He was so used to coming out on top he never worried excessively about anything. His mother attributed his fortunate constitution to the rare Roxidant herb she'd consumed when she'd been pregnant with him. Whether that had anything to do with it was hard to say. The fact remained - he was one of a rare breed of lucky people.

Sumo's body lay at the foot of the doors. Phil opened both of them and resumed the push to get rid of him. The fresh air outside was welcome.

"Push him over that way a bit more and we'll leave him to sleep it off. He'll be safe next to the window," Joc said.

"Sotty asked us to bring him home," Kam reminded Joc.

"We can't take him anywhere. He'll be fine. Sotty can pick him up in the morning. No one will touch him. He stinks."

"That's true."

"One more push oughta do it. Should we leave him on his back or put him on is side?" Joc expressed an ounce of thoughtfulness.

"Better leave him on his side in case he chucks," Phil suggested.

"We'll haffta balance him up against the wall then, face forward, otherwise he'll topple over." There was Joc's nice streak again. Twice in thirty seconds. That had to be a record.

The guys rolled Sumo into position. His inert body lay at a sixty-degree angle to the wall. Satisfied that he was not going to roll onto his back, the guys filled their lungs with fresh air and went back into the bar where Sumo's odour lingered.

"Kenny, fresh drinks all 'round," Phil called. "Keep putting them on the old man's tab. You having one Marc?"

Marc was feeling sick. He could never remember a time when he'd felt so bad. He lay on the floor moaning.

"Joc, you gotta let me out of the suit. I'm gonna die." His voice was strained and feeble. A bit of a put on maybe, but he needed the extra effect.

Joc looked at him and felt bad - for a split second. He walked over to Marc and knelt down. "OK, you've had enough."

He pulled the laserweld from his pocket and flicked the switch to reverse. Marc rolled painfully onto his back so the zip was fully exposed. Joc aimed the gadget and pressed the button but nothing happened.

"That's odd. The battery must be dead. Mmm. Sorry, there's nothing I can do for you."

"Get another battery, you sexless neuter."

"Another battery. That's a good idea. I bet E.P.'s got a spare. I'll go and ask him."

Joc got up, moseyed back to the bar, took a long sip of his drink and strolled off to find E.P.

Marc knew right then he had no intention of letting him out of the suit. What did he expect? That his night out would have a fairytale ending because that was the way it was supposed to be.

He had to accept that he was the sucker for the night and whatever would be, would be. Sumo had taken all his shit with surprisingly good grace and Marc had enjoyed watching him suffer. And suffer he had. It was time to suck it up and get on with it.

"Phil," he called, "get me a Frozen Summer."

Slowly Marc pulled himself up and with his arse cheeks squeezed tightly together, waddled to the bar.

Joc returned. "Marc, you're up! Phil, the cruiser's ready."

"That was quick. E.P. is one mover and shaker."

"Did you get a new battery," Marc asked.

Joc clicked his fingers. "Battery! I knew I went out there for something. Must be all the booze that's made me forgetful." He reached for his drink, finished it off and ordered another.

E.P. came into the bar. "You'd never even know the cruiser had been touched," he announced to Phil brightly. "It looks better than new. Try and avoid crash landings in future - the under carriage needed straightening out. Those Zippy Mowers took a bit of time, but they're as good as new. I checked on Harri and he's sleeping like a baby. I expect you won't see him for a while."

"How'd you fix everything so fast?" Phil asked.

"Trade secret my boy. If everyone knew, then everyone'd do it too. Am I right or am I right?"

"You're right."

"Kenny, a round of drinks for the guys and I feel like singing," E.P. suddenly declared.

E.P. sat down at the piano and sang a song about a pair of shoes.

"Pity Harri's not here. He'd appreciate this tune," Tash said.

"Everybody sing," E.P. yelled with a flourish.

They sang. Marc sang. All that was left for him to do was wait for the big moment and it was coming on strong and fast now. The noise helped to block out some of the pain so he sang louder and encouraged the others to do the same.

Over the noise of the music and voices, Marc's stomach made itself heard. Everything went quiet for an instant. Marc's eyes squinted up, his face went a deathly white and he gasped loudly. Quick as a flash, E.P. changed the tune. To the strains of 'Ain't that a Shame', Marc filled his boots.

Epilogue

Earth's papers were full of dozens of claims about UFO sightings. It would seem from all the stories being bandied about that a fleet of aliens had come to Earth and tried to take it over. It was amazing how one cruiser with a bunch of guys on a buck's night could suddenly become a cast of thousands who were threatening the very fabric of society.

Everyone who was trying to be someone got their two cents worth in. Money was being paid out hand over fist for every exclusive that came a publications way. The woman on the aeroplane was writing her life story. Hollywood was already casting the lead parts. Donny made the most of his new found fame and made up an outrageous story about abduction and all its alleged horrors. Hollywood beckoned him. He compromised his artistic integrity for the money and quit the play.

The photo Bruce had taken came out looking like a grey, fuzzy blob. The lights on the cruiser had run together in a blur and were indistinguishable. It was printed anyway because it looked no better or worse than any of the other photos that were floating around, complete with a vivid tale of terror describing their close encounter - compliments of Linda.

Even Sergeant Tyler had a story to tell because he decided what had happened to him had been the work of extra-terrestrials - which indeed it had been - but he was only guessing. The donut chain immediately changed their advertising slogan. It now read - 'Aliens love our donuts'.

Business was brisk.

Most of the people who had actually encountered the guys were none the wiser about who they'd been dealing with. Herb and Pammy, who were still together and sharing the pain of Herbie's cruel rejection from Juilliard, never figured it out, neither did Bernardo and his boys. Billy from the disc shop never remembered anything for longer than five minutes so the guys weren't even in his head anymore. He couldn't explain the missing discs and was promptly fired. He got a job working behind the reception desk at an airport motel.

The traffic cops in England were too busy trying to explain how they had gotten alcohol soaked vomit on themselves to worry about getting in on the alien thing. They were accused of drinking on duty and scored themselves another year on traffic duty.

A group of alien 'experts' denounced the Yorkshire farmers flattened wheat as a poor attempt at trying to raise funds by exploiting the curious and gullible nature of people. Once the word 'hoax' was used, people stayed away in droves.

Code Red and Zero Care who, it turned out, had been the ones trying to rip off the cruisers hubcaps before it so rudely vanished, kept very quiet. Normally they would have welcomed the extra cash their tale would have brought, but they were wanted by the police. Any publicity would have been most unwelcome, especially seeing as they were committing a crime at the time of the strange event. Really, they were lucky to be alive anyway because they'd nearly killed each other trying to open the beer.

So what began as a perfectly innocent night of fun for a group of out-of-towners ended up in a flurry of speculation and insinuation that planet Earth was no longer a safe place to be and that next time - the aliens just might stay.

The only ones who remained unconcerned about what they'd seen were the sheep in New Zealand, and Sugar Anne. For some reason she felt no need to cash in on the hype and, really, she was the only one who had a legitimate tale of horror and abduction to tell. She finished her book and continues to wait, and wait, for a reply from the publisher she submitted it to.

Phil's old man loved 'Voyager'. It was placed in the front garden as an ornamental piece. Naturally it became a talking point amongst the neighbours, who were incredibly jealous. To date, he hasn't figured out that it opens and contains within it a wealth of saleable stuff.

The tough chicks from Amazonia were eventually rescued from the Rubbish Tip by a group of grotesque, one-eyed, hairy, dump pirates. After five frustrating weeks of trying to escape from the suffocating stench of rotting food that was so strong it practically ate the paint off the Starbuster, the girls had all but given up hope. Every direction they flew in eventually brought them back to the point at which the vacuum had originally deposited them. They flew fast, slow, up, down, left, right, sideways, all ways - it didn't matter, they were trapped with absolutely no means of escape.

On one particularly hot day the girls decided if they didn't find a way out before another two weeks was up they would crash the ZX into a pile of hideously ugly furniture that had no right to have been designed and built in the first place. They were figuring out the speed they should be going when they made impact, so they would be sure to die quickly and painlessly, when Lynara saw someone pick up one of the brown, tile top coffee tables the girls intended to crash into.

Sticking her head out of the window and shrieking loudly at the person to leave their suicide pile alone, Shabon and the others assumed for a moment she had gone completely mad until they looked up and saw the table being loaded onto the back of a trailer which was laden down with other bits of useless junk.

The girls wasted no time in making contact with the dump pirates. In exchange for helping them load their trailer to overflowing, the girls were guided out of the Rubbish Tip and back to an area of space they were familiar with. The dump pirates were only too glad to show them the way out because they didn't want anyone snaffling any of the treasures that the Tip housed.

Over all their very long days, the girls had vowed endlessly that they would search the ends of the universe until they found the guys who had forced them into the depths of hell and they had decided E.P.'s was the place to start looking because, before the race, they'd heard Davis mention that was where the guys had to be. They intended to torture anyone they had to until they discovered the identities and whereabouts of the bastards in the cruiser.

The moment the girls were released from their living nightmare they headed at breakneck speed towards E.P.'s.

And they were very, very pissed off.